FROM
WONDER
TO
WISDOM

DR. KHALID SOHAIL

EDEN KHAWAJA

2025

Copyright

Published in 2025 by Green Zone Publishing
A division of Dr. Sohail MPC Inc.
213 Byron St. South
Whitby, Ontario Canada L1N 4P7
T. 905-666-7253   F. 905-666-4397
E-mail: welcome@drsohail.com
Website: www.drsohail.com

From Wonder To Wisdom
Khalid Sohail, 1952 –
Eden Khawaja, 2008 –

1. Biography   2. Psychology   3. Philosophy

ISBN: 978-1-927874-74-5

Cover Artwork: Huma Dilawar

Cover Design: Vicky Chen

Textual Design: Marcelina Naini

Unexamined life is not worth living.

~Socrates

Table of Contents

INTRODUCTION

Dr. Khalid Sohail

I have known Huma Dilawar and Zubair Khawaja for nearly a decade. We have been meeting to have delicious dinners and intellectually stimulating dialogues. During those meetings Huma shared her poems and Zubair shared his political ideas and ideals. I also shared my humanist philosophy.

During those meetings I also met their daughter Eden Khawaja, who was a shy little girl. Then I heard that she wrote short essays for her school. When I asked her to share them with me, she would ask her mother to read them to me as she was painfully shy.

In 2025 when there was a book launch of my auto-biography *Saalik*, that was the Urdu translation of my autobiography *The Seeker*, Huma said that Eden had expressed a desire to read the English version. So, I gave Eden a copy of my autobiography as a gift and jokingly said that I would like to read her comments after she had read my book. She smiled and said, "Sure". At that time, I did not think that she would oblige. But I was wrong. After she read the book, she sent me the following review of *The Seeker*.

Khizr's journey is both external and internal, a deep exploration of what it means to come fully alive. The narrative is not simply in the telling but sees each encounter as a metaphor for challenging convention. Khizr's forced moment of awareness about the unfulfillment of his own life acts as a catalyst, forcing him not only to question conventional thinking but also the automatic habits that have a tendency to leave us bound within the societal conventions of our ascribed lives. As we read along, we are introduced to a shift that is intimate and universal. The writing of Dr. Khalid Sohail is typical in its simplicity and compactness. This is a style that makes us pause and reflect on our own life, on the choices we have made and the aspirations we have not followed. Therefore, the book is not only an autobiography or a story but an invitation to look at the subtle patterns of our existence. The reason the book is so captivating is that it is written in allegory. Khizr's life is not a straight, one-way path but is woven with symbols and metaphors, which echo on a higher level. Whether it's the imagery of existence as a string of moments or the voyage of rediscovering self, each bit of information is meant to cause readers to think. Not just does this make reading more intriguing but also equips readers with the chance to embark on their own journey of self-discovery, questioning everything from social norms to the daily routines that structure existence. Furthermore, the narrative demonstrates the redemptive power of questioning. By having the courage to question what is routinely taken for granted, Khizr recovers the freedom to define his own future. His story is a reminder that true development often begins with the courage to step outside our comfort zones and challenge the limits imposed on us by others' expectations. The book offers an honest self-remembering, a gentle but unrelenting invitation to surrender yesterday's habits and embracing a wiser, and more contemplative life. In one sense, of course, The Seeker is nothing more or less than one man's evolution; but at a deeper level, it's an offer each of us receives to look inside ourselves and remember the unimagined possibilities of transformation. It challenges us to see life not as a stiff chain of events that are ruled by convention but as a changing tapestry, open to being rescored in the colours of our own choosing. Whether you're at a crossroads in life or simply in need of a fresh perspective, this book is both mirror and map that invites you to question, set out, and, ultimately, live more authentically.

Zubair told me that Eden enjoyed the English version of The Seeker far more than Huma and Zubair liked the Urdu version, Saalik. Zubair congratulated me that my book had crossed three generations as I was seventy-two and Eden was only sixteen.

I was pleasantly surprised. I felt as if my story had created a literary connection between a writer and a reader. After a few days I got a letter from Eden asking me if she could call me Gruncle [shorter version of Grandpa Uncle]. At that time, I realized that Eden felt an affectionate emotional connection with me that was stronger and deeper than just a literary connection.

After that special connection we started exchanging letters that were personal as well as philosophical. That was a new experience for me. I was amused and amazed. I had not realized that Eden had become so wise at such a young age. I am sure alongside her own readings and self-reflections there was also an influence of her creative parents. Eden was lucky to have a family environment where her both parents had serious dialogues with her about different social, political and philosophical traditions.

I was further surprised to know that a shy teenager, who hardly said a few words in our family meetings, was so expressive in her letters. I thoroughly enjoyed exchanging letters with her. It gave me an opportunity to articulate my personal, professional and philosophical ideas and ideals.

These letters are a testimony that a genuine dialogue can take place between different generations. Now when I jokingly say that I am fortunate to be friends with Eden, her mother Huma and her father Zubair, the *unholy trinity*, we all laugh.

I hope our readers enjoy our letters as much as we enjoyed writing them.

Peacefully,
Dr. Khalid Sohail
2025

LETTER NO. 1 — GRUNCLE

Dear Gruncle Sohail,

I remember you once asked me how I came up with the name "Gruncle Sohail." The truth is, over the past few years, I've grown closer to you, and like I do with the people dearest to me, I felt the need to give you a name that carried warmth and familiarity.

As a kid, I was obsessed with Gravity Falls, a show full of mystery, adventure, and a weird sense of humour. One of the characters was Gruncle Stan: a gruff, cynical, and self-serving man. The funny thing is, you're the complete opposite of him. Where he's hardened, you're kind; where he looks out for himself, you're endlessly generous. What started as a playful nod to a childhood show quickly became something much more meaningful.

I believe I have seen a lot in this world, but nothing has lifted my parents' spirits quite like your kindness has. And for that, I'll always be grateful. I often think back to my younger self, the one who once insisted she could never be your friend because you seemed too perfect. But even now, I wouldn't call you a friend. You're something far more lasting. You're family.

From the moment we met, you've supported my writing, my thoughts, and my dreams. You've never spoken to me like I was just a kid but as a person in my own right, someone worth listening to. The simple act of calling me Eden instead of defining me by my parents gave me a confidence I never thought I'd have. In this messy process of figuring out who I am and what I want to be, that kind of recognition means more than I can say.

And beyond all that, you're a reflection of the kind of future I hope to have: a psychiatrist in a cozy apartment, helping others while still making time for creative passions. You live in a way that's both humble and extraordinary. I can only dream of feeling that kind of happiness and peace, because right now it feels so out of reach.

So I have to ask, how do you stay a humanist when humanity itself can be so cruel?

Love,
Eden

LETTER NO. 2 — HUMANITY AT A CROSSROADS

Dear Eden,

From the first time I met you a few years ago, I was impressed by your intelligence and creativity. You sounded far more mature than your age. I wanted to have a dialogue with you but the problem was that you were painfully shy. So I had to wait till you felt relaxed and comfortable with me to start discussing different subjects on your own initiative.

Finally, when you read my autobiography *The Seeker* and wrote a wonderful and insightful review, I thought the ice was melting and there was a connection. Your dad also told me that you enjoyed *The Seeker* more than he enjoyed its Urdu translation titled *Saalik*.

I was pleasantly surprised when I got your message stating,

"I was wondering if we have reached a point in our friendship where I can call you Gruncle Sohail (grandpa-uncle). Is that okay with you?"

And my spontaneous response was, "My honour"

Dear Eden, when I read your letter explaining how you came up with the title Gruncle Sohail and shared that you felt like a little person rather than a kid in my presence, it reminded me of a page of my diary that I want to share with you as it relates to my loving grandma my sweet Nanny Jaan. I hope you like it. In my life she was the first person who treated me like a little person.

MY LOVING GRANDMA SARWAR

When I think of my childhood, the first image that comes to mind is the kind face of my maternal grandma that I called nanny jaan. Nanny jaan was a beautiful woman. I remember her fair complexion, dark short hair and brown eyes. She used to wear shalwar, qamees and dupatta and did her household chores quietly. In winters she used to wear a Kashmiri woolen shawl. She was graceful, reserved and elegant. Underneath her calm surface, she was an ocean of love. She was full of caring and compassion, warmth and affection. I never saw her angry, resentful or bitter. I never saw her yelling, screaming or shouting at her children and grandchildren.

She was a wise woman.

She listened more and talked less.

She was a woman of few words.

She was not a poet but knew the power of words.

She was not a mystic but knew the value of silence.

She was not a therapist but knew the significance of listening.

For me she was a goddess of love.

Some of my fondest memories of my childhood are my visits to 4 Mozang Road, Lahore during summer vacations. Whenever we went to visit her, she used to hug me and kiss me on my forehead. She used to offer me choices.

Would you like to have apple juice or coke?

Would you prefer hot or cold milk?

Would you like to sleep downstairs or upstairs?

She was always very thoughtful. She was the first adult who made me feel like a little person, a special human being and I loved it. I felt closer to her than my own mother. I was so fond of her that I dedicated my collection of stories *Mother Earth Is Sad* to the fond memory of my late grandma, my loving and wonderful nanny jaan.

Dear Eden, at the end of the letter, you have asked me a question,

So I have to ask, how do you stay a humanist when humanity itself can be so cruel?

To answer that question satisfactorily and in detail one needs to write a whole book. I can only give you a brief answer.

I believe in human evolution and the journey of evolution is slow very slow, like a turtle even slower than that like a snail.

The journey is also not in a straight line.

Three steps forward, one step back

Two steps forward one step back

Human beings have an average age of 70 years so they get easily frustrated and disappointed.

Evolution happens in centuries.

I am an eternal optimist. I believe human beings are evolving and growing and learning through their mistakes.

Let me give you just one example. Human beings have understood the significance of human rights. The United Nations has passed a resolution announcing a Declaration of

Human Rights. It will take a few centuries before communities and countries put that in action.

Let me share one more page from my book *The Next Stage of Human Evolution,* that might help you understand my philosophy of life.

....

HUMANITY AT A CROSSROADS

In the 21st century, humanity is going through adolescence. If we compare evolution of humanity with the personal growth of one human being, we can see that a two or four-year-old child is not mature enough to commit suicide. But when a child reaches adolescence and becomes a teenager, he or she can commit suicide and some do. But most teenagers choose life over death and live through their turbulent adolescence. Similarly, humanity is also going through that turbulent and distressing adolescence. In the 20th century, for the first time in history, humanity was able to commit collective suicide by nuclear weapons and other weapons of mass destruction. In the 21st century humanity has a choice: to commit collective suicide or grow to the next stage of human evolution and learn to live in harmony and resolve their personal, social, religious and political conflicts peacefully. Let us hope humanity chooses peace over war, love over violence, wisdom over ignorance.

Dear Eden, now it is my turn to ask questions?

Is it true that you want to become a psychiatrist or a psychologist or a therapist?

What inspired you to dream of becoming a mental health professional?

Affectionately,
Gruncle Sohail

LETTER NO. 3 — MENTAL HEALTH CARE WORKER

Dear Gruncle Sohail,

You asked me why I want to become a psychiatrist, and truthfully, I'm still figuring that out myself. In today's hyper-competitive academic world, becoming a doctor feels almost like chasing a mirage, so instead, I'll use the term mental healthcare worker. To me, it encompasses psychiatrists, psychologists, psychotherapists, neuroscientists, and neurologists alike.

My love for science began early. I've always believed that all children are born curious, but it's their parents who shape how that curiosity blooms. Mine nurtured it with endless patience, always explaining things in a way that my young mind could understand. Simple enough to grasp, yet scientific enough to be true. This early exposure to pure knowledge became the foundation for how I see the world.

As I grew older, my questions matured. "Why is the sky blue?" turned into "How does the theory of evolution disprove the existence of God?" By six, I was questioning the militant authoritarianism of Pakistan's government. By eight, I had begun to understand that we live in an oligarchy masked under the blanket of what we believe to be democracy. And then came a question I couldn't answer, one that felt bottomless. Why do people strive for power?

I didn't find an answer, but I found something better. Psychology. I hadn't even known it was a field of science. At that age, science was neatly boxed. Biology for living things, chemistry for substances, and physics for forces. But psychology cracked something open in me. The idea that human behaviour could be studied, mapped, and understood through the lens of the mind, shaped by experience, relationships, and even genetics felt nothing short of revelatory.

Through this curiosity, I stumbled upon mental illnesses. And then I found depression. The symptoms felt eerily familiar, as though someone had transcribed my inner world. Could I really be depressed? But how? I was just a child. One who was loved, cared for, and surrounded by friends. What could I possibly have to be sad about?

Back then, I didn't recognize it as trauma. But slowly, my world began to collapse. I was so young, yet certain I wouldn't live to see twenty-five. At nine, I started self-harming, digging my nails into my palm until it bled, and eventually cutting myself with a pair of small scissors hidden in my drawer. My parents noticed, of course. They took me to our family doctor, and then to several psychologists. At ten, I was diagnosed with depression, and for the first time, I felt like my pain had a name. That I wasn't just being dramatic or seeking attention. I was unwell, and it was real.

Which brings me back to your question, why I want to become a mental healthcare worker. I want to help diagnose children before their pain metastasizes into something unmanageable. I want to expand our understanding of childhood mental illness beyond just ADHD, Autism, or Dyslexia, to include anxiety, depression, and the quieter suffering that often goes unnoticed.

I can't promise to fix everything. But I can be a presence, a voice, a support. I can help people make peace with their past without guilt or shame. And maybe, just maybe, I can help keep one child from feeling as alone as I once did.

I hope this wasn't too much, or too personal, but I wanted to be honest with you. And I hope it answers your question. Now my question for you is, is there any ultimate truth in the universe, and if there isn't, what's the closest thing you've discovered to it?

Love,
Eden

LETTER NO. 4 — CREATING A MEANINGFUL LIFE

Dear Eden,

Reading your letter I had mixed emotions.

On one hand I felt sad that you went through such emotional turmoil at such an early age. I had no clue that you suffered so much.

On the other hand, I felt glad that you have transformed your breakdown into a breakthrough. That shows your resilience and your commitment to recovery and healing. That also explains why you matured so early because you were able to absorb your emotional experiences in your personality.

I am so glad that you want to become a mental health worker to help other suffering human beings. You will be a wonderful therapist and people will be lucky to have you as their healer.

You have asked me if there is 'an ultimate truth in the universe"?

Religious people believe there is an ultimate truth as God created this universe and revealed that ultimate truth to humans by prophets and scriptures and human beings are expected to follow divine revelations to discover that ultimate truth.

Being a secular humanist, I do not believe there is an ultimate truth in the universe as I do not believe in organized religions. I consider religions as part of mythology and scriptures as part of folklore. Their stories are folktales. I think human reason is more important than divine revelation. I am of the opinion that human beings created the image of God rather than God creating human beings.

Since there is no ultimate truth, human beings are free to discover their own truth individually and collectively and create a meaningful life for themselves.

Over the years and decades, I have made my life meaningful by recognizing that I have a creative personality and choosing a creative lifestyle that consists of

Creative psychotherapy

Creative writings

and

Creative friends.

I have discovered that when ordinary life experiences are impregnated with meaning they transform into extraordinary existential encounters.

I discovered two secrets of a meaningful and purposeful and successful life and they are passion and compassion. My passion is expressed in my creating writings and my compassion is expressed in my creative psychotherapy. I am lucky to have a family of the heart, that includes your family, who share my creative interests and hobbies and my dreams of creating a peaceful world.

A few years ago I did a small study on that subject and wrote an essay. I am sharing that essay with you hoping that it would shed some light on that subject. I hope you like it.

....

CREATING A MEANINGFUL LIFE

In the last few years a number of people who struggled emotionally because of the meaninglessness of their life, came to my clinic to consult me as a psychotherapist. They did not suffer from any mental illness. They were not psychotic or clinically depressed. Their main complaint was,

"My life is meaningless"

"I have no purpose in life"

"My life is not fulfilling".

They wanted me to help them in creating a meaningful life.

While I was working with these people in therapy I prepared a questionnaire and sent it to my friends and colleagues to find out how they discovered their meaning in life. I thought reading those responses might help and inspire my patients to create their own unique meaning in life. My questionnaire included the following four questions.

1. *Do you believe LIFE has a meaning? If yes, what is it?*

2. *Does YOUR LIFE have meaning? If yes, what makes it meaningful?*

3. *Did you ever feel YOUR LIFE was meaningless? If yes, how did you make it meaningful?*

4. *Do you consider yourself a religious, spiritual or a secular person? What is your philosophy of life?*

....

I was pleasantly surprised by the enthusiastic responses. Those responses ranged from 5 lines to 5 paragraphs to 5 pages. Interestingly in the respondents there were more men than women and more secular than religious people. When I read all the responses I received I realized that their answers could be divided into the following groups.

1.   *MEANINGFUL PERSONAL DREAMS*

A number of respondents had personal goals, ambitions and dreams that made their life meaningful. As they followed their passions and dreams their life took a positive turn and made it more enjoyable. Some wanted to develop their fullest potential while others wanted to develop their artistic talents and create masterpieces.

One respondent said, "One must live one's life to the fullest...ensuring one is true to oneself first and foremost..."

One artist responded, "Until I have created my 'masterpiece' there will be a void, but perhaps that is the pursuit of many artists."

A writer stated, "I read books, I write books, which makes life very meaningful."

One respondent quoted George Eliot who said, "It is never too late to become what you might have been."

2.   *MEANINGFUL RELATIONSHIPS*

There were a number of respondents who found meaning in their emotional bonds. For them their friends, sweethearts, spouses, colleagues and relatives enriched their lives. One mother said, "My children make my life meaningful..." For many, loving relationships were a source of meaning in their lives.

One respondent stated, "What makes life meaningful is the fact that I have a family, have children, grandchildren, friends, relatives...."

3.   *MEANINGFUL SERVICE TO HUMANITY*

There were a large number of respondents who believed that serving other human beings made their life meaningful. Their altruistic behaviour helped them rise above their selfish mindset and made them part of the whole humanity. They felt they were part of creating a happy, healthy and peaceful world. One respondent said, "My life has meaning because I care about other human beings. I have been involved in human rights issues since I was a teenager and I have been trying to educate people about that. Another task that I have taken upon myself is to encourage people to adopt scientific thinking and I have been quite successful in that. Those endeavours make my life meaningful. They make me feel that I HAVE made a difference."

4.   MEANINGFUL CONNECTION WITH GOD AND RELIGION

There were a small number of respondents who felt that their special relationship with their God and religion provided a meaning to their lives. One respondent who suffered from depression believed that belief in God helped many depressed people to stay alive otherwise those who felt desperate would have committed suicide. He stated, "…in case of depression, it is religion that gives you support and a light for living, otherwise there should have been much more suicides in the world than those occur at present. Everyone gets depression at one time or another. Some overcome it without any help, some need psychiatric help. Religion, right or wrong, provides good psychiatric support to overcome depression and provides a meaning to life and the urge to live." One female Muslim stated, "I have always felt the presence of ALLAH around me and that has always been meaningful to me."

Another male Muslim wrote," So I am a Muslim and believe in One God, the Creator and the concept of life after death and accountability of my actions in this existing life. And this assumption or faith has made my life meaningful."

Does Life In General Have Meaning?

In my interview alongside asking people about their personal life I also asked them whether life in general had a meaning. Most secular people believed life had no intrinsic meaning while spiritual and religious people believed life had an inherent meaning. Some seemed unsure. One woman said "Life has a meaning but I do not know what it is". Some believed it SHOULD have a meaning otherwise life would be meaningless and the idea of a meaningless life made them uncomfortable. One respondent stated, "Every life must have had a meaning, for if not, then the whole act of creation becomes meaningless..."

It was interesting for me to see how for some religious people a faith in God and religion and for spiritual people their spiritual ideals made their lives meaningful. One Muslim stated, "My life has a meaning to serve ALLAH and be able to connect people with ALLAH". On the other hand secular people did not need God, religion or spiritual values to make their lives meaningful. For them their art, music, loving relationships and serving humanity were enough to lead an enjoyable, exciting and meaningful life. For some secular people their spirituality was more connected with humanity than divinity. One secular respondent said, "I am a very spiritual and secular humanist. The source of spirituality is love, knowledge and above all music."

Some secular people had a unique perspective on the meaninglessness of life. One stated, "I find the meaningfulness of life in its meaninglessness." Another non-religious person felt meaning was not important to enjoy life. He said, "…overall I find my life most satisfying—whether with or without meaning"

Some secular people believe that as human beings evolve and grow and develop rational and logical thinking, their need for God and organized religions will become less and less. One respondent stated, "God was created by humans for psychological and emotional reasons. As human courage and wisdom grows further, God will be buried in the caves he came from"

It was fascinating to see how secular people searched for meaning in life without religious and spiritual traditions. One quoted Bertrand Russell for defining good life, "A good life is one, inspired by love and guided by knowledge." The other responded that he tried to make his life meaningful by, "Enjoying various thrills of life that nature has gifted us, with the least amount of guilt and repentance. He added, "I am extraordinarily conscious of my cosmic ignorance and I strive to be compassionately ego-less, carefully fearless and ethically guilt-free."

SERVING HUMANITY

Of all the religious, spiritual and secular respondents, alongside their differences of opinion, they had a reasonable consensus on one aspect. Most of them agreed that serving humanity was a major source of making their lives meaningful as such activities connected them with other human beings in a meaningful way.

One respondent said, "…One of the major pleasures is to be of some help to other human beings…" Such behaviours decrease human suffering and increase quality of life. Serving humanity creates genuine bonds and friendships between people where they rise above the religious, cultural, gender and ethnic differences and connect with common humanity. It seems as if by serving humanity human beings can strive to become fully human individually and collectively, rise to the next stage of human evolution and become part of creating a loving, just and peaceful world.   One of my favourite responses was, "My aim is to be the best person I can be and to strive to change the world for the better even in a small way."

When I was reviewing the responses I realized that some people had accepted the traditional meaning of life, the meaning offered to them by their families, communities, religions and cultures, while there were others who had rejected the traditional meaning but found their own meaning to their lives.

When I shared the responses with the people I was working with in my clinic who were struggling with meaninglessness in their lives, as it was distressing for them, they found those answers quite helpful. It offered them hope and inspired them to discover their own unique meaning by:

...focusing on their personal talents and pursuing a hobby, a passion and a dream. They finally got in touch with the special gift life had offered them but they had been unaware of it

...developing new relationships and creating a circle of close friends, that I call *family of the heart*

and

... doing some voluntary work to serve their communities.

I was pleased that my friends sent thoughtful answers to my questions and I felt honoured that my patients gave me an opportunity to help them in creating meaningful lives. Helping them also gave meaning to my life as a humanist psychotherapist.

Dear Eden,

Now it is my turn to ask two questions.

How do you see yourself different from your classmates and people of your age?

How do you cope with those differences?

Peacefully,
Sohail

LETTER NO. 5 — HERD MENTALITY

Dear Gruncle Sohail,

I've always believed that all questions are important, that there's no such thing as a bad question. But there's one that has stuck with me, and not in a good way. It's one I've been asked countless times, and each time, I never quite know how to answer it: How are you different from others your age? It's similar to the question you asked me, and if I'm being completely honest, my instinctive answer is: I'm not.

At least, that's what I used to think.

I don't believe anyone should be considered different just for the sake of being different. There's no universal guide to being a teenager. No mould we're all supposed to fit into. We're all just figuring it out as we go. Just like adults, teenagers hold a wide range of beliefs and perspectives, even if they sometimes come off as naive because of our lack of life experience.

I've met classmates who fit the classic teenage stereotype. Moody, disrespectful, and self-absorbed. But I've also met teenagers who are thoughtful, humble, and honestly wiser than many adults I know. Some of them have a surprisingly deep understanding of politics, economics, and literature. That said, those kinds of people are rare.

And as I'm writing this letter, I'm starting to realize something: maybe I am a little different. Not completely, but enough to notice.

In one of the first articles I ever wrote, I explored the idea of the "herd mentality", how people often follow trends and social norms without questioning them, like sheep in a herd. And now that I reflect on it, there are quite a few things I don't follow. I don't drink or smoke. I don't go to parties. I don't wear makeup every day or only wear branded clothes. I don't listen to pop music or watch the latest Netflix shows everyone else is talking about. None of these things make me better or more interesting…they just make me — me.

My interests in cultural anthropology, leftist politics, health sciences, and art are a strange but honest mix of what I was exposed to growing up. Part of it comes from my parents' influences; the rest is a result of my own curiosity and passions. I guess you could say that just as artists shape their work in the image of their own defiance, so too did my unconventional parents shape a child in the spirit of their unorthodoxy.

The second part of your question asked how I cope with my uniqueness. But the truth is, I've never really felt like it was something to cope with. Each individual is a unique blend of similarities and differences, since no one is ever a perfect mirror or a perfect contrast to another.

I have friends I share music tastes with. Others I connect with through politics or psychology. But interestingly, my best friend shares none of those interests. We don't like the same music, we don't agree on politics or religion, and we barely have any mutual hobbies. Yet, she's like the sister I never had. Our bond goes beyond surface-level things. It proves to me that real friendship isn't about having everything in common. It's about feeling safe and understood around someone.

High school is a weird time. Everyone is awkward. Everyone is unsure of themselves. So my own awkwardness never really made me feel like an outcast. In fact, I've always felt relatively safe among my peers, because deep down, I think we all know we're in the same boat. Just a bunch of hormonal teenagers trying to find ourselves while quietly crumbling under the pressure of expectations and the looming fear of the future.

So now, instead of asking, how am I different, I've started asking more essential questions: What does it mean to live authentically in a world that rewards performance over presence? Is authenticity a fixed trait, or is it something we continually construct. Moment by moment, choice by choice? And maybe the hardest question of all: Am I brave enough to live with the discomfort that often accompanies truth?

It's strange how clarity and uncertainty can coexist. I'm clearer now about who I am, but no less aware of how fragile that understanding is. I've come to believe that authenticity isn't a destination, it's a discipline. It requires constant negotiation between the self I know and the self I'm still discovering. Between the desire to be accepted and the need to be whole.

And maybe that's where I'd love to hear from you. When you were my age, did you ever feel torn between the need for belonging and the responsibility of self-honesty? Did you ever feel like you were carving a path that hadn't yet been drawn, while everyone else seemed to walk along one already paved and approved? What gave you the courage to keep walking, especially on days when the silence felt louder than the applause?

Love,
Eden

LETTER NO. 6 — CHALLENGING SOCIAL CONDITIONING

Dear Eden,

I am so impressed that your first essay was about 'herd mentality'. There are so many people around us who never become aware of the effects of social, religious and cultural conditioning on their personality and philosophy. No wonder they follow the path of their parents in religion as well as politics.

That is why…

Children of Christian parents become Christians in Canada

Children of Muslim parents become Muslims in Pakistan

and

Children of Hindu parents become Hindus in India.

You have asked about my experiences as a teenager and as a young adult. Let me share a few interesting encounters with life.

There was a time I used to live near Eid Gah in Peshawar. One evening I saw hundreds of people praying in the evening on Eid Gah. I was surprised as it was not Eid day and I knew that Eid prayers are performed in the morning.

I asked an old man, we called Baba Ji, why they were praying? He said they were offered Special Prayers [*namaz e istisqa*] for rain as it was very hot and people were dying of heat stroke.

The next day I asked my science teacher if people could create rain by praying. My teacher laughed and said,

"Rain and sunshine are caused by laws of nature and not by prayers."

So, I waited and waited and waited for three weeks but there was no rain.

Then I met Babaji again and asked him why it did not rain?

He said, "People who prayed were sinners and God only listens to the prayers of pious people."

That was the time I started to doubt the religious teachings and what role God played in human lives.

When I was fifteen my mother asked me to follow the teachings of the Holy Quran to become a good Muslim. Since I did not understand Arabic, I went to different libraries in town and brought Urdu translations of the Quran by five well respected religious scholars. For the next five years I seriously studied translations and explanations of the Quran by five scholars. I realized that they did not agree on any major issue.

For example, some scholars did not believe in Darwin's Theory of Evolution and believed it contradicted the Quranic story of Adam and Eve while other scholars accepted Darwin's Theory and believed there was no contradiction between teachings of Quran and Darwin's Theory of Evolution.

There was no way for me to know what the correct meanings of Quranic verses were.

So at the age of 20, I said goodbye to God and organized religions.

When I told my poet uncle Arif, who was a socialist at that time, that I have said goodbye to God and religion, he suggested that I keep quiet about my religious beliefs or lack of them and wait till I graduate from the medical school and then go to some Western country and live there with my atheistic ideas.

I was amused when my uncle told me,

"Your uncle's uncle became an atheist at the age of 60

Your uncle became an atheist at the age of 40

and

Now you have become an atheist at the age of 20.

You are following your family tradition."

My uncle Arif also introduced me to the concept of

Traditional Majority that follows the highways of tradition

and

Creative Minority that follows the trails of their hearts.

Later on, I developed that concept further and wrote a book titled *Creative Minority*.

If you have not read that book, I can present it to you as a gift. That book will show you that you also belong to the Creative Minority.

People belonging to the Creative Minority have non-traditional philosophy and personality and lifestyle. That is why they get into conflict with traditional schools and colleges and communities and have to face serious emotional and social problems. Some even have nervous breakdowns. I studied the mysterious relationship between creativity, insanity, sexuality and spirituality.

In every generation we have poets and philosophers, scientists and scholars, artists and mystics, reformers and revolutionaries who belong to this Creative Minority. They are in minority, but they lead the traditional majority to the next stage of human evolution.

Trails of one generation become the highways for the next generation.

Villains of one generation become the heroes of the next generation.

Now a question for you.

When you think of the future, how far do you think?

What are the creative dreams for your future?

When I was a teenager, I had four dreams. If you are interested, I will share with you those dreams in my next letter after reading your creative dreams.

Affectionately,
Gruncle Sohail

LETTER NO. 7 — FUTURE DREAMS

Dear Gruncle Sohail,

You ask me how far ahead I see when I think about the future, but I've never really been one to dream in centuries. I think about the future the way some people think about the countryside. Far enough to feel like a destination but close enough to imagine the roads.

For me, that means around 15 years from now. I'll be in my early thirties. The age where childhood starts to feel like a story someone else told you, and the age when the choices you made in your teens come back either as blessings or debts. I imagine myself waking up in an apartment I chose for myself somewhere in a big city. Not a mansion, nothing flashy, just a space that feels safe. There might be plants, like vines of English Ivy adorning the walls, with posters of my favourite metal bands along with them. Hopefully, none of these plants are dead. Maybe a partner, their gender not mattering to me, who knows how to make iced coffee the way I like it. Maybe not. I don't think the presence or absence of a romantic partner defines the success of a life, especially not a life as simple as mine.

I'd like to think I'll be doing something that matters. Writing, maybe, maybe not. Or creating something with impact. Something people can carry with them after they leave my psychiatric clinic. But at the same time, I've never been interested in the idea of legacy.

As for creative dreams...I'm still figuring out what that even means for me. I've always felt things deeply, noticed details others miss, thought in metaphors without meaning to, but I'm not sure if that qualifies as creativity, or just sensitivity dressed up. I sometimes wonder if I have anything original to say, or if I'm just echoing smarter people in slightly different words. I know I want to make something. Something honest. But I'm not sure what form it will take. Maybe writing, though I'm constantly second-guessing my voice, and sometimes even writing feels like a burden. It's strange to feel like you have a lot inside you, but no clear way to let it out. Like carrying around a story in a language you haven't learned yet.

Lately, I've been wondering if I've been putting too much pressure on myself to be extraordinary. To have the next big idea or write something brilliant or create work that everyone remembers. But the truth is, most days, I don't feel like a visionary. I feel like a person who's just curious about the brain, about why people do what they do, about how emotion and memory shape the way we live. And maybe that's enough.

Maybe it's okay if I never write a ground-breaking book or launch some revolutionary project. Maybe being devoted to understanding the mind, and trying to help people feel less alone in theirs, is a quiet kind of creativity too.

I used to think that in order to matter, my life had to be filled with remarkable achievements. But I'm starting to realize that meaning doesn't always look like accolades or applause. Sometimes it looks like showing up. Like studying something you love just because it fascinates you. Like noticing how light moves across your room at 4 p.m. Or being the kind of person a friend can cry with on a random Tuesday. Maybe those small things are their own kind of legacy. The legacy I yearn for.

Now here's a question for you. When you were 30, did you feel like yourself yet, or were you still trying to figure out who that self even was? How does that tie in with the four dreams you had as a teenager?

Love,
Eden

LETTER NO. 8 — FOUR DREAMS AND FOUR CHALLENGES

Dear Eden,

I am enjoying this exchange of letters as through these letters I am getting to know you better and I am also able to reflect on my biography and philosophy, my dilemmas and dreams, my struggles and successes and draw LOL...*lessons of life.*

Your letter reminded me of a seminar of the Family of the Heart in which I shared my reflections of my dreams and the challenges I had to face to fulfill those dreams. I think you will find it interesting.

FOUR DREAMS and FOUR CHALLENGES

My Creative Journey from age 16 to 61
Family of the Heart Seminar December 15th, 2013

Ladies and Gentlemen,

A couple of weeks ago when the invitation of the seminar was circulated I asked myself, "What would I like to share with you people in this seminar?" The first thought that came to my mind was that the city of Toronto has played a significant role in my creative journey. My creativity was the seed, and the literary atmosphere of Toronto was the fertile soil in which the creative seed turned into a plant and grew to be a tree and produced literary fruits in the form of poems and stories and essays and interviews and books and documentaries in Urdu as well as English. It is still a mystery for me how I started as an Urdu writer in Pakistan and transformed into an English writer in Canada. So I want to publicly acknowledge the role Toronto, my creative and humanist friends of the Family of the Heart, and my creative colleagues of Creative Psychotherapy Clinic, that include Anne Henderson and Bette Davis, played in my literary, creative and philosophical growth.

When I reflect on my past as a writer, humanist and a psychotherapist, I realize that quite early in life I fell in love with literature, art and philosophy and I realized that they could be useful in discovering my truth, inspiring others and serving humanity. When I reflect on my life- long love to serve humanity I remember two couplets, one of Faiz Ahmed Faiz and the other one of Arif Abdul Mateen.

The first couplet is

Faiz thi raah sar basar manzil

Huma jahan pohunchay kamiyaab aaye

[Faiz, every step on the way was a destination

we were successful wherever we were]

And the second couplet is

Bas aik saboot apni wafa ka hay meray paas

Main apni nigahoN main gunahgaar nahi hooN

[I have only one proof of my love and faithfulness

I am not guilty in my own eyes]

At an early age I also realized that all creative people, whether poets or philosophers, artists or mystics, painters or playwrights, scientists or scholars, reformers or revolutionaries, psychologists or psychotherapists, have a creative personality and a creative philosophy that guides them in their creative expression and creative communication. They have profound and deep love in their hearts for humanity. Khalil Gibran once wrote, "Don't you ever think you can guide love. If love finds you worthy she will guide you." I feel fortunate that love for humanity has been guiding me. It helped me overcome my fear that I expressed in my short poem titled

APPREHENSION

I am afraid
The noise of the outside world
Will drown one day
The music inside.

I realized that love was closely connected with creativity and creativity was intimately connected with freedom. I became aware that there were two kinds of freedom, inner freedom that dealt with freedom of thought and imagination and outer freedom that dealt with freedom of expression and action that was intimately connected with the limitations, restrictions and inhibitions imposed on the creative personalities by their conservative families, communities and cultures. Success of the creative personalities depended on how they kept their inner music alive and how they coped with outer limitations. Let me share with you a few highlights of my creative journey from the age 16 to 61.

When I was a teenager I became aware that my life was a special gift that nature had given to me. I asked myself, 'How can I make my life meaningful and successful? What would be the best use of this special gift?" So I came up with four dreams about my life.

The first dream was to become a doctor and a specialist. I thought I would serve humanity better as a psychiatrist than a family physician, as I would be able to help my patients and their families, in their emotional suffering that can be more painful than physical suffering. I think watching my father have a nervous breakdown as a child and my mom looking after him must have unconsciously influenced me to become a psychiatrist. I wanted to study until the age of 30 and then serve my patients for another 30 years and then retire. At the age of 16 I could not imagine living more than 60. This is an interesting coincidence that I received my FRCP in psychiatry 3 weeks before my 30th birthday in 1982. After getting my Fellowship I served as a psychotherapist in different hospitals and clinics for 30 years. So now at the age of 61, I can say that I successfully fulfilled my first dream.

My second dream was to become a writer and write a series of books. As a teenager I was impressed by writers like Saadat Hasan Minto and Ismat Chughtai, Sigmund Freud and Carl Jung, Vladimir Lenin and Mao Tze Tung. All of them had created a body of work. They were like marathon runners and I wanted to develop the attitude of a marathon runner rather than a 100 meter sprinter. So, for the last forty years, I have been consistently writing and I have been successful in creating more than 40 books. So my second dream also came true.

My third dream was to travel the world. Rather than reading the books of History and Geography I wanted to visit different parts of the world and meet people of different cultures and see how they lived. So after receiving my Canadian Passport in 1982 I went to Israel and South Africa, two countries to which I could not travel on a Pakistani Passport. After that I traveled in North America and South Africa, Latin America and the Middle East and visited Russia and the Scandinavian Countries. Of all the countries I traveled to, three cities that inspired me the most were Jerusalem, Paris and Athens as they were full of history and art and mythology. After the 9/11 tragedy, traveling was not as enjoyable as before but I felt that I had already fulfilled my third dream.

My fourth dream was to create a circle of creative friends. After meeting Ashfaq, moving to Toronto, and getting involved in the publication of *Urdu International*, I met many creative friends like Jawaid Danish in USA, Abrar Hasan in France, Saeed Anjum in Norway, Nasar Malik in Denmark, Sain Sucha in Sweden, Yousaf Hasan in Pakistan and Zahir Anwar in India. I interviewed many scholars who visited Canada from India and Pakistan including Kishawar Naheed and Fehmida Riaz, Sharib Rudoulvi and Gopi Chand Narang, Abdullah Hussain and Saqi Farooqi and many more.

After I published my book *From Islam to Secular Humanism*, I met many humanist friends from different religious and cultural backgrounds and presented papers in many Humanist seminars and conferences. So I fulfilled my fourth dream also.

While I was fulfilling my dreams I realized that I, like many other creative personalities, had to face different challenges and overcome different obstacles before I could be successful. I can share four challenges that I can identify. In Urdu they can be named as *rawayat, hijrat, dualat and shohrat.* [Tradition, migration, wealth and fame]

The first challenge was tradition. My family wanted me to have a traditional marriage and live a traditional family life. I realized quite early that if I wanted to be a successful writer and therapist, I had to choose a non-traditional lifestyle. So I did not choose a traditional family life. For me, family life was a fulltime job and being a writer and a therapist was also a full time job and I could not do two full time jobs in my lifetime. I know many creative people who tried to keep a balance between two full time jobs and finally left both of them unfinished and incomplete.

The second challenge was migration. Very early in my life I had realized that my creative personality and non-traditional philosophy was incompatible with the traditional, conservative and religious environment of Peshawar, Pakistan. When I, at the age of 20, confessed to my poet uncle, Arif Abdul Mateen that I had become an atheist, he told me that he had also become an atheist at the age of 40 and his uncle, my grandfather, that I met later on, had become an atheist at the age of 60. He suggested that I keep quiet about my rebellious religious views, leave the country after my graduation and move to a secular country where I could practice what I believed. So I went to Iran and then came to Canada to study and to live. If I had stayed in Pakistan, it is quite possible that I would have been assassinated or sent to jail or landed in a mental asylum.

My dear friend Rasheed Nadeem has a couplet

Ye shehr agar zarf kushada nahiN rakhta

main bhi yahan rehnay ke irada nahi rakhta

[If my city is not broad minded and does not have a big heart, then I have no intentions to stay here]

The third challenge was wealth. There are so many doctors and lawyers and engineers and businessmen who are obsessed with money. In my life I have had to sacrifice materialistic gains for the sake of my ideals of serving suffering humanity and my community. I chose to become a psychotherapist and have my own clinic and treat my patients to the best of my ability rather than becoming rich. Serving humanity was dearer to me than becoming a millionaire. That was the third challenge I had to face for my ideals.

The fourth challenge was fame. I have met many writers and artists who chose fame over art. For them public relations and appearing in newspapers and radio and TV interviews became more important than their creativity and literature and art. I always focused on my new book and new project. I know many contemporary writers who have reached their creative menopause and have stopped writing and creating. I feel lucky that even at the age of 61, I feel young and enthusiastic and creative. I am always planning my next story and my next essay, and focusing on my next book. And in that process of planning my new creations my creative friends have always been a great inspiration.

In the end let me share with you a folktale that deals with freedom needed for creative personalities to survive and thrive. I heard that folktale as a child and it has remained a source of inspiration all my life.

The folktale is about a wolf and a dog. The wolf used to live in a jungle and enjoyed his freedom. When he was young, he was healthy and happy and energetic and he had no problem running fast and catching his prey. But when he got older and weaker he became afraid that he might not be able to catch his prey and starve and die a desperate and miserable death. One day while he was walking on the outskirts of the jungle, he met a healthy and handsome and well-nourished dog. He asked the dog the secret of his happiness. The dog said that he had a master who fed him and kept him in his house. The wolf asked the dog if he would introduce him to his master and the wolf could spend his old age with them. The dog had no problem and asked him to come to the same place the next day to meet his master. When the wolf heard that promise he became happy and hopeful about his future for a few seconds.

But when the dog turned around, the wolf saw some hair was missing on his neck. On asking, the dog shared that his master had a bad temper and when he was angry, he used to chain the dog in the basement for a few days. Missing hair was a reminder of the chain. Seeing the missing hair and hearing the dog's story, the wolf reflected for a few seconds and then withdrew his request to meet the dog's master.

That folktale of the free wolf and the chained dog has guided me on many occasions when I faced personal, professional and existential dilemmas in my life. I always identified with the struggling, but free wolf, rather than the well-nourished, enslaved dog. I believe our freedom inspires us to face challenges and offer sacrifices for our ideals and make our lives meaningful. I feel fortunate that I could embrace my freedom and I was able to love, create and serve.

Thank you!

....

Dear Eden,

I have discovered that I have a Creative Personality and my creativity makes my life meaningful, purposeful and successful. My creative lifestyle consists of a creative triangle.

Creative Psychotherapy

Creative Writings

and

Creative Friends

I have also discovered two secrets of happiness

Passion

and

Compassion

My passion is expressed in my creative writings and sharing them with my creative friends and my compassion is reflected in my creative psychotherapy with my patients and their families.

Affectionately,
Gruncle Sohail

LETTER NO. 9 — FREE WILL

Dear Gruncle Sohail,

A few weeks ago, I remember Mama sending me an article you had written in Urdu. I was confused at first as to why she asked me to read an article in a language I couldn't read, but then I saw her text: "Translate the article into English. It's by Dr. Sahib, so I know you'll enjoy it. Read the comment under it as well." I was curious, so I did just that. I was pleasantly surprised to find out that your article was about free will. I love the topic, as it reminds me of one of the greatest opportunities I have been given: the United Nations Young Leaders Training Programme.

In one of the modules, we had a lesson about free will. An entire eight hours of lectures and debates on the topic, with people from all over the world and from different walks of life discussing what they believed free will to be, and whether we had it. It reignited my passion for questioning and debate. Despite writing a response to one particular comment beneath your article, I wasn't satisfied with what I wrote. The complex discussion of free will deserves a much more detailed and academic essay, so that's what I'll be writing.

The question of whether we have free will has long challenged scientists and philosophers, and as new research emerges, we seem to be settling the idea. Although there is no consensus in the philosophical debate yet, progress in brain science has now reached the point where some understanding of how one's own will, freely determined, might be implemented in the brain has become possible. As evidence continues to accumulate, it appears that free will is not the illusion I was originally led to believe, but is generated by the brain's ability to represent, evaluate, and execute a critical subset of actions in a flexible, goal-oriented way.

At the heart of this investigation is the prefrontal cortex, an area of the brain responsible for higher-order abilities, including planning, decision-making, and the suppression of impulsive behaviour. It's this space where various threads of information, such as sensory stimuli, memories, or emotions, come together to evaluate choices and select potential actions. The dorsolateral prefrontal cortex, in particular, is critically involved in the conscious control of behaviour, allowing people to wait for gratification, overcome habitual responses, and align decisions with long-term goals. Its importance lies at the core of what is commonly referred to as the subjective experience of being free during action.

Of particular note are the neuroimaging and electrophysiological findings that neural activity associated with decision-making may occur even before conscious intention to act becomes apparent. Experiments, including those of Benjamin Libet, reveal a readiness potential in the brain milliseconds before one reports the conscious decision to move. Although some have taken these findings as a challenge to free will, recent interpretations describe these early signals as the accumulation of potential courses of action rather than the unequivocal selection of a decision. Conscious awareness may act as a final gatekeeper, capable of endorsing or vetoing impending actions, a process referred to as "free won't."

Moreover, the brain's default mode and executive control networks collaborate to simulate future outcomes and reflect on past experiences, both essential for autonomous choice. This reflective capacity enables individuals not only to react but also to deliberate, imagine alternatives, and make decisions that reflect personal values and goals. The variability in decision-making, even under similar conditions, underscores a degree of freedom that is not easily reducible to simple causation.

Now that the neurological aspect is out of the way, it's critical to address the anthropological and philosophical sides of this discussion. From an evolutionary standpoint, early hominins benefited from flexible decision-making. The capacity to choose among multiple behavioural strategies allowed for better survival in variable environments. This rudimentary form of agency laid the groundwork for more complex forms of deliberation.

As humans evolved greater cognitive capacities, they developed a sense of self-reflection and foresight, essential elements of what we now describe as free will. In small-scale societies, this cognitive flexibility became essential for navigating social dynamics. Making choices that balanced individual desires with group norms was crucial for maintaining cohesion. Thus, the evolutionary pressures of social living helped scaffold the psychological underpinnings of perceived autonomy.

Human free will cannot be disentangled from the development of symbolic thought. Archaeological evidence from early Homo sapiens, such as cave art, burial rituals, and tools, points to the emergence of abstract reasoning and intentional planning. These behaviours indicate not only a capacity for foresight but also a growing awareness of agency. Unlike other primates, humans began to perceive themselves as actors within a symbolic order, capable of reflecting on alternatives and choosing among them. This internalization of decision-making processes marks a key evolutionary step toward what we now understand as free will.

Rituals and language are essential to expressing and negotiating free will. Initiation rites, for example, often involve symbolic choices that mark a transition in social status and personal responsibility. Language, too, allows for the articulation of intent, doubt, and alternatives. Linguistic structures that presuppose the existence of agency. The capacity to say "I could have done otherwise" is not a given in all species; it is a product of complex sociolinguistic development.

A critical anthropological dimension of free will is moral agency, the ability to distinguish right from wrong and to act accordingly. Among hunter-gatherer societies, for instance, norms around sharing and reciprocity were enforced not through formal law but through social sanction and praise. These mechanisms suggest a shared expectation that individuals can choose to align, or not, with communal values. Anthropologists argue that the sense of personal responsibility, foundational to free will, emerges within such socially embedded contexts.

From a philosophical perspective, free will is the idea that individuals have the capacity to choose among alternatives and act upon those choices meaningfully. On a metaphysical level, the concept of free will depends on the idea of agency, where individuals are the true initiators of their actions. Libertarian philosophers argue that not every event is causally determined by prior conditions of the universe. Instead, they propose that certain actions stem directly from the agent, who exercises a non-deterministic capacity for choice. This view is rooted in the theory of agent causation, which holds that individuals are not simply links in a causal chain but are themselves originators of new causal sequences.

In contrast, compatibilists argue that free will can exist even within a deterministic universe. Philosophers such as David Hume and, more recently, Daniel Dennett contend that free will doesn't require the absence of causation but rather the ability to act in accordance with one's own internal states. Such as desires, beliefs, and intentions, without external compulsion. From this perspective, what matters is not randomness at the metaphysical level but the authenticity and self-governance of one's choices.

Existentialist philosophers such as Jean-Paul Sartre advocated the radical freedom of the human subject. Sartre argued that humans are "condemned to be free," meaning that freedom is not optional but intrinsic to human existence. For Sartre, even inaction or submission is a form of choice, and with this freedom comes inescapable responsibility. This existential account emphasizes the lived experience of making choices, the anxiety that accompanies freedom, and the authenticity that arises when one accepts this condition. From this perspective, denying free will is a form of bad faith. A refusal to confront the burden and dignity of human freedom. On the other hand, Karl Marx viewed free will not as an abstract, individual capacity existing in isolation, but as something deeply shaped by material and social conditions. He argued that human freedom is constrained by the structures of economic and class relations within society, particularly under capitalism, where individuals are often alienated from their labour and subjected to systemic inequalities. For Marx, genuine free will could only be realized when individuals are no longer dominated by these external forces, especially those tied to private property and class exploitation. In this sense, true freedom is collective and material: it emerges through the transformation of society toward communism, where people have control over the conditions of their lives and labour. This view stands in contrast to Jean-Paul Sartre's existentialist perspective, which emphasizes radical individual freedom and personal responsibility regardless of external circumstances. Sartre believed that individuals are always free to choose, even in oppressive or limiting situations, and that they bear full responsibility for their actions. While Marx focused on how social and economic structures limit freedom, Sartre saw such constraints as challenges to, but not eliminations of, human agency, highlighting a fundamental clash between structural determinism and existential autonomy.

Moral responsibility relies on the existence of free will. Without the freedom to choose their actions, it becomes difficult to hold individuals accountable, whether through praise, blame, punishment, or reward. Thinkers such as Immanuel Kant argued that morality is grounded in autonomy, maintaining that the idea of moral law loses its meaning unless people can act freely and rationally. In addition, ethical frameworks rest on the assumption that individuals possess the capacity for reflection and self-regulation. The ability to consider options, recognize duties, and commit to principles all point to some level of volitional freedom. Absent free will, ethics collapses into a deterministic model of stimulus and response, stripping it of its normative power.

Your thoughts on free will sparked a cascade of memories, ideas, and insights, connecting my experiences in the United Nations program with centuries of philosophical and scientific exploration. Delving into free will through the lenses of neuroscience, anthropology, and philosophy has only deepened my appreciation for how complex and essential this topic truly is. Whether understood as a biological function, a social construct, or a metaphysical concept, free will remains central to our understanding of human nature and moral life.

Thank you, Gruncle Sohail, for reigniting this passion in me. I'm looking forward to continuing the conversation, perhaps over chai and some lively debate soon.

Now I want to ask you a question.

Is monogamy a societal construct or a biological tendency?

With a heart full of love and curiosity,
Eden

LETTER NO. 10 — FREEDOM

Dear Eden,

When I read your letter, first I was amused that you gave such a powerful answer to the reader who criticized my blog that he became speechless. After reading your response he must be lost for words as he did not pursue the debate any further.

After being amused then I was amazed that you wrote such a scholarly letter about free will. You brought the biological, psychological, social and philosophical arguments together. In spite of being a multi-dimensional essay, there was one dimension missing and that was the personal dimension. So in my response I will bring personal and philosophical dimension together so that it reflects bio-sophy, a combination of biography and philosophy so that if one day we publish our letters the readers will find them more engaging and interesting. I will divide my response into many segments to address many aspects of freedom.

(1)

When I think of all of the memories and experiences that shaped my philosophy about *freedom*, the first image that comes to my mind is one from my early childhood, when I was maybe three or four years old. Even now as an adult, when I close my eyes I can see myself with my tricycle, standing in front of a closed door with a metal bar in our house in Kohat, Pakistan. I want to open the door to go outside but I cannot. The bar is too high for me to reach. I can hear children playing in the street. I want to play with them but I cannot. I look at my mom with pleading eyes and ask,

"Mom, can you open the door?"

"No, I cannot."

"Why not? I would like to go out and play."

"No, it is not safe. What would I do if they kidnapped you? "

Disappointed, I walked away. The longer I listen to the sounds of the children playing, the more frustrated I feel. My mom, seeing me sulking, says "Wait, till your dad comes home. He will take you out for a bike ride."

That image of me standing at the closed door is etched in my mind. I remember that when my mom was not around, I tried many times to open the door, but I could not. I felt like a bird in a cage.

Now that I think about my life, I feel that the images of the closed door and the metal bar and the feeling of helplessness have stayed with me all these years. Maybe those feelings have helped me empathize with people held behind metal bars and closed doors, whether Eastern women forbidden to leave home, or writers and intellectuals imprisoned for their writings or psychiatric patients kept in hospitals or prisons against their wishes.

I sometimes feel that my empathy is not only for human beings but also for cats, dogs and birds kept as pets, locked up in the house or in a cage and not allowed to play with their friends and mates.

Whenever I think of that image, I remember the story of a parrot in Toronto whose owner wanted to go to India to visit his family. He had brought that parrot from India with him to Toronto. Before leaving for India, he asked his wife and children what gift he could bring back. He then asked his parrot if there was anything special he wanted him to do while he was traveling in India. The parrot asked him to visit his friends there and wish them the best and ask for their advice for him. At the end of his trip he went to see the parrot's friends. When he gave them the message from his parrot, he was shocked to see that one of the parrots fell from the tree and died.

When the owner returned, he gave gifts to his family and then related the story to his parrot. Upon hearing the story, the parrot fell off his perch and died. The owner, dismayed at the death of another parrot, took the cage outside, opened it and dumped out the bird. The moment the parrot touched the ground, he opened his eyes and flew to a nearby tree.

"Why did you do that?" the owner asked in bewilderment.

"I was acting on my friend's advice," the parrot responded.

"What advice?" The owner was still puzzled.

"My friend sent the message that to be free you have to die. Death is the price one has to pay for freedom."

I sometimes wonder whether that is why one of the values closest to my heart has been freedom, be it the freedom to travel or freedom of speech, financial freedom or emotional freedom, social freedom or political freedom.

That first image of the closed door and metal bar has been a mixed blessing for me, creating pain as well as a sense of empathy for all living beings behind closed doors and metal bars, whether humans, animals or birds.

(2)

In my professional life as a psychotherapist, when I encourage people to be spontaneous and creative and explore their potential, I am surprised by the reasons they give me that they cannot do that. They have adopted ideologies that curtail their freedom and increase their limitations and sufferings. I call them deterministic doctrines. Some have adopted:

A. Genetic Determinism. Such people believe that their genes have already decided their personality and their future, and they are going to suffer because their parents and grandparents suffered.

B. Psychic Determinism. Such people believe that their childhood experiences, over which they had no control, have eclipsed their lives and that they will never be able to enjoy anything.

C. Social Determinism. These people believe that since they were born into a certain tradition and culture, they are unable to do certain things and adopt certain lifestyles as they would be persecuted and penalized for them.

D. Religious Determinism. These people believe that their lives have been predetermined by God who has already written in a holy book [loh-e-mehfooz] how all human beings are going to live their lives from birth to death. It is their fate and they are unable to change it.

E. Astrological Determinism. Such people believe that their lives depend upon their date of birth and the configuration of the stars when they were born. Since they had no control over the time of their birth and the stars, they have no control over their future.

F. Spiritual Determinism. Such people believe in the phenomenon of re-incarnation and explain their tragedies by their past lives.

I am amazed that all such people are preoccupied with what they *cannot do* rather than what they *can do*. I believe human beings might have all those biological, psychological, social and cultural predispositions and inclinations, but they are not controlled by their instincts like birds and fish and animals as they have a choice *to act or not to act* on those biological influences, psychological messages and social temptations. At each stage of life human beings can change their course and choose to follow a different path. American psychiatrist Harry Stack Sullivan, father of interpersonal psychiatry wrote, *"Your emotional life is not written in cement during childhood. You write each chapter as you go along."*

I believe human beings have a duality in their nature. They have a choice to become the most violent or the most peaceful human being. They are free to choose and that freedom is part of their nature, their humanity.

In my clinical practice as a therapist, I encourage people to review their conditioning and their deterministic ideologies, get in touch with their creative self and do things that they like to, want to and love to do and in this way they enhance their freedom and spend more time in a healthy, happy and peaceful state of mind. I encourage them to get in touch with their goals and ambitions, desires and dreams, and then make those dreams come true.

(3)

When I lived in the oppressive environment of Pakistan, I was familiar with only one kind of freedom. I wanted *freedom from* all the chains of restrictive traditions. But after I left the East, and came to the West, I realized that there was another kind of freedom, which is *freedom for*. At one time I knew only what I did not like or want, but I had no idea what I liked or wanted in my life. I knew what philosophy I rejected, but I did not know what philosophy I wanted to follow. I met many other men and women who knew what kind of relationships they did not want to have, but had no clear idea what kind of relationships they wanted. I was in that no man's land for a few years. Then I discovered the road, the philosophy and the lifestyle that I was comfortable and happy with. In my books I have shared my journey

...from traditional family to the family of friends that I call Family of the Heart

...from traditional religion to the philosophy of humanism

...from the traditional psychiatric practice based in psychiatric hospitals to the Green Zone humanistic psychotherapy in my Creative Psychotherapy Clinic

...from traditional writing to creative writing by integrating my biography with my philosophy. I continued to explore different forms of poetry and essays, interviews and letter writing, focusing on the themes closer to my heart and mind.

(4)

Over the years I have realized that many of those who fight for freedom of speech and action do not realize the significance of freedom of thoughts and creative imagination. They do not appreciate that freedom is a state of mind. People can be free in the most oppressive and suppressive environments. Victor Frankl discovered that freedom in concentration camps and in his book *Man's Search for Meaning* acknowledged it in these words, "…everything can be taken from a man but one thing; the last of the human freedoms…to choose one's attitude in any given set of circumstances, to choose one's own way…it is the spiritual freedom…which cannot be taken away…that makes life meaningful and purposeful." Gradually I am realizing that my freedom of thought has to be translated into freedom of action to make my life successful and meaningful.

After becoming a Secular Humanist, I asked myself how I would define "good" that is not based on religious beliefs derived from heavenly scriptures. I liked the secular definition of "good" offered by Bertrand Russell. He suggested that a good action is the one that is

Inspired by affection, caring and love

and

Guided by knowledge, experience and wisdom.

As a secular humanist I also wanted to define my ego-ideal, the concept of an ideal human being, and exercise my freedom to actualize that. In my sixties I feel that an ideal person is the one who has

...the mind of a scientist that enjoys logical, rational and critical thinking

...the heart of an artist that has a keen sense of aesthetics and creates beautiful things

and

...the personality of a mystic that is kind, so that people feel peaceful when they are in his company.

Such a person

...would have developed higher consciousness and would be willing to serve humanity whenever the need arises.

...would be at peace with himself and in harmony with his environment.

...would value other people's freedom as much as he values his own freedom at a personal, social and political level.

Such a person would be caring and creative and compassionate. I strive in my humble way to become such a person. As opposed to Sartre's philosophy that *we are condemned to be free*, my view is that as human beings we are fortunate to be free to become fully human individually and collectively, to use our freedom to create a peaceful world together and to make our tomorrows better than our yesterdays.

Dear Eden,

I hope you liked my letter. Now you are free to share your personal experiences with freedom in your family and community.

Peacefully,
Gruncle Sohail

LETTER NO. 11 — LOVE, SEX AND MARRIAGE

Dear Eden,

You have asked me what I think about Monogamy. It is not easy for me to answer your question in a few sentences. I have thought a lot about that subject and written a whole chapter about it in my book titled

Sexual Fantasies and Social Realities.

In this letter I will share a few pages of that chapter. In my book I have included autobiographical stories and interviews to support my views. After reading these pages if you are still interested I can send you the PDF copy of the book to read those stories.

Intimate Relationships — A New Bio-Psycho-Social Classification

Some people have sexual encounters but never fall in love, while others fall in love but never get married, and then there are others who had arranged marriages and lived with their spouse all their lives but never fell in love. All these scenarios show us that sex, love and marriage do not have to coexist in the same relationship. With the discovery of the contraceptive pill and social and cultural changes more and more people have been experiencing freedom in their romantic lives and are able to make choices in the 21st century that were not possible a couple of centuries ago.

Based on my professional experiences working with people with sexual and relationship problems and my reflections on the literature published on the subject, I have devised a classification that can help us understand the psychology and dynamics of intimate relationships. Because each human being is unique and each intimate relationship is mysterious and changes with time and maturity, we need a classification to have a meaningful dialogue about such serious aspects of life. Since sex has been a taboo in many cultures, we do not have words, expressions and terms to describe different shades of our personality. I have created new expressions as I found existing terms unsatisfactory. In some cultures the expressions single, unmarried and celibate are synonymous, reminding us of times when they meant the same thing. But now we can have single people who are not celibate and celibate people who are married. We need to have an open dialogue to clarify some of this confusion. The classification I am presenting is based on the bio-psycho-social model acknowledging different aspects of human personalities and lifestyles. It highlights that:

Biological and instinctual drives that we share with animals are expressed in sex.

Psychological needs, wishes and dreams are expressed and shared in love.

Social needs, obligations and expectations are expressed in marriage in which law, religion and culture play a major role.

Human beings, all their lives, try to balance their biological, psychological and social needs, and their dilemmas and dreams. That balance changes with life experiences and level of maturity. This classification has the following groups of people.

SEX

1. *ASEXUAL PEOPLE.*

These people have no or very low sexual desire. Because of lack of desire, they do not engage in sexual behavior or sexual relationships. As compared to asexual people, celibate people have a desire but do not act on that desire. Some of them are shy and introverted and have psychological reasons for celibacy while there are others who are celibate for spiritual reasons as they associate sex with sin and celibacy with holiness.

2. MONO-SEXUAL PEOPLE.

These people have sex with one person. Some of them associate their sexual behavior with love and marriage.

3. BI-SEXUAL PEOPLE.

These people have sex with two people. These bisexual people are different from those bisexual people who have sex with both sexes. One does not exclude the other.

4. POLY-SEXUAL PEOPLE.

These people have sex with many people. It can be part of having many spouses or just different sexual partners as a single person.

LOVE

5. A-PHILOUS PEOPLE.

These people never fall in love with any person. They are usually shy and inhibited or live in a remote place where the availability of partners is very limited.

6. *MONO-PHILOUS PEOPLE.*

These people fall in love with one person at a time. Some get involved sexually while others never have sexual contact with the person they are in love with. Sometimes the other person does not even know about the intensity of the intimate feelings.

7. *BI-PHILOUS PEOPLE.*

These people fall in love with two people at the same time. Some act on their desires and fantasies while others keep it a secret. When relationships are open, partners might have to deal with the issue of jealousy.

8. *POLY-PHILOUS PEOPLE.*

These people fall in love with many people at the same time. Some have the courage and opportunity to share those feelings with their loved ones while others share their feelings with only one and keep their feelings for others a secret.

MARRIAGE

9. *A-GAMOUS PEOPLE.*

These people never marry any person. Either they do not believe in marriage, or never have an opportunity to marry because they cannot find a suitable life partner.

10. *MONO-GAMOUS PEOPLE.*

These people marry one person at a time. They are usually traditional people who cherish the tradition of monogamy.

11. *BI-GAMOUS PEOPLE.*

These people marry two people at the same time. In some countries it is legal if the first wife gives her blessing. Some men use the first wife's apparent infertility as a reason.

12. *POLY-GAMOUS PEOPLE.*

These people marry many people at the same time. It is amusing that in many cultures a man having multiple wives is socially and legally acceptable but a woman having multiple husbands and becoming polyandrous is not acceptable. There are some cases in India where three brothers married one woman as they had to share the money to pay for the dowry. Each one of them independently could not afford a spouse.

According to this classification many traditional men and women who live in lifelong monogamy are mono-sexual, mono-philous and mono-gamous.

People who have married one person but have sex with many will be mono-gamous but poly-sexual.

People who are married to one but fell in love with many but never had sex with them would be mono-gamous but poly-philous.

This classification also highlights that people's social behaviors are not true reflections of their fantasies and nature which is more complex and complicated than what appears on the surface. We need to have open and honest dialogues about love, sex and marriage so that we can have better insights into the human condition in order to make wise choices in matters of the heart.

A NEW BIO-PSYCHO-SOCIAL CLASSIFICATION

BIOLOGICAL	PSYCHOLOGICAL	SOCIAL
SEX	LOVE	MARRIAGE
ASEXUAL	APHILOUS	AGAMOUS
MONOSEXUAL	MONOPHILOUS	MONOGAMOUS
BISEXUAL	BIPHILOUS	BIGAMOUS
POLYSEXUAL	POLYPHILOUS	POLYGAMOUS

Dear Eden,

I hope my classification is not confusing. You are more than welcome to ask questions and share your thoughts about my ideas about sex, love and marriage.

Affectionately,
Gruncle Sohail

LETTER NO. 12 — MY TRUTH

Dear Gruncle Sohail,

Thank you for sharing such a thoughtful and intellectually rich framework for understanding love, sex, and marriage. Your classification system offered a compelling lens through which to view the multifaceted nature of human intimacy, and it provided language for experiences I have felt or observed in others but previously struggled to articulate.

I found your separation of the biological, psychological, and social dimensions of intimacy particularly illuminating. Too often, these aspects are conflated or assumed to be naturally aligned. Your model challenged that assumption and encouraged me to consider the ways in which cultural narratives shape our understanding of relationships. This brought to mind Michel Foucault's assertion that "sexuality is not just about bodies and desires, but about discourses and institutions." His work emphasizes that even our most intimate experiences are mediated by broader sociocultural forces, a point your framework powerfully reinforces. Anthropologically, this is echoed in the work of scholars like Margaret Mead and Bronisław Malinowski, whose ethnographies reveal the profound variability in sexual norms and relational structures across cultures, underscoring that what we often treat as "natural" is in fact deeply contingent on historical and cultural contexts.

From a biological perspective, your framework's acknowledgment of the decoupling between sexual desire, romantic love, and long-term attachment reflects findings in evolutionary psychology and neurobiology. Research has shown that these three systems, lust, attraction, and attachment, are governed by different neurochemical pathways (e.g., testosterone, dopamine, and oxytocin, respectively), which can operate independently or in tension. This lends further credence to your model, which does not assume a unified trajectory of intimacy but instead allows for fluid, intersecting pathways of connection.

Your terminology, such as "poly-philous" and "mono-sexual but poly-philous," further deepened my appreciation for the diversity and complexity of human relationality. These distinctions reminded me of Robert Sternberg's Triangular Theory of Love, which conceptualizes love as comprising three components: intimacy, passion, and commitment. Notably, Sternberg's theory posits that these components can exist in varying degrees and combinations, much like your own model, which offers a more nuanced understanding of how individuals might navigate love and desire in non-normative but deeply meaningful ways. From an anthropological standpoint, this aligns with evidence that different societies prioritize different components of Sternberg's triangle, some emphasizing communal responsibility over romantic passion, or pragmatic partnership over emotional intensity.

What I found most compelling, however, was the tone of your writing. It was strikingly nonjudgmental, marked by intellectual rigor without moral prescription. This, to me, is an essential quality of any meaningful discourse on intimacy. As Bell Hooks so aptly wrote, "Love is an action, never simply a feeling." In that sense, the action of love includes creating space for others to define and express their truths without fear of judgment or erasure. Your framework embodies that ethic by prioritizing understanding over conformity. This openness resonates with the anthropological principle of cultural relativism, the idea that one must understand behaviours and beliefs within their own cultural context rather than through the lens of one's own norms.

I also share your belief in the importance of open, shame-free conversations about topics that remain taboo in many cultural contexts. As Esther Perel has argued, "The quality of our relationships determines the quality of our lives." By encouraging dialogue rooted in curiosity rather than condemnation, your work contributes to a much-needed shift in how we think about relational well-being. Biologically, this is crucial as well social connection and secure attachment have been shown to have profound effects on both mental and physical health, from lowering stress levels to increasing longevity. Your model, by fostering more authentic and accepting forms of connection, is ultimately a blueprint for both emotional and biological flourishing.

Reflecting on your letter about freedom led me to consider my own relationship with the concept of freedom, particularly as it relates to identity, expression, and interpersonal connection. This is a subject of profound personal significance to me, and I recognize that much of my capacity to explore and embrace my full self stems from the unwavering support I have received from my family and close friends. Their encouragement has been instrumental in my emotional, intellectual, and spiritual development.

From a young age, my parents cultivated a sense of autonomy in me. They not only permitted independent thought but actively nurtured it. Intellectually, they welcomed difficult questions and encouraged me to form my own beliefs. Emotionally, they allowed space for vulnerability, teaching me to express and understand my feelings rather than suppress them. Creatively, they supported my explorations in writing, music, and art without imposing expectations or conditions. This holistic support system instilled in me a strong sense of self, grounded in both independence and connection.

It is from this foundation that I began to question and eventually understand my identity more fully. I distinctly remember encountering the word *queer*, being curious about its meaning. There was a lesson about it in school, and we learned the struggles some people faced in regards to opening up about it since it was still considered a taboo subject. As I had done with many topics before, I approached my parents with a question that was, in retrospect, deeply significant: "Hypothetically, what would your response be if one day I said that I was queer?" My mother's immediate, unhesitating response was, "However you are, you're still my daughter", offering a profound reassurance that would remain with me for years to come. From my mother's side, I had unconditional support and freedom, but my father's response was a bit more different. His support was conditional, conditional to my age, which I now understand was an important aspect for my self-identity and growth as it taught me that some things come with age and experience, and that being 'too young' is a real thing.

As I entered adolescence and began to recognize my queerness not merely as a theoretical construct but as an intrinsic part of my identity, that early moment of acceptance proved foundational. The process of coming out was not fraught with fear or shame; it was, in many ways, an affirmation of the freedom I had always known. When I eventually disclosed this part of myself to my mother, her loving and almost nonchalant response, "So why are you telling me this? This doesn't change the fact that you still have to become a doctor", was humorous and underscored what I had always sensed: that my worth and identity were never contingent upon conformity to external expectations.

In reflecting on these experiences, I have come to understand freedom not merely as the absence of constraint, but as the presence of acceptance. It is about being recognized and supported in one's full humanity, even when that humanity deviates from normative scripts. My experience of freedom has cultivated in me a deep sense of resilience, empathy, and authenticity. It has informed the way I relate to others, the way I think, and the way I love.

Thank you again for sharing your work and for providing such a meaningful contribution to the ongoing dialogue around intimacy and identity. Your insights have enriched my understanding and inspired me to continue engaging with these themes both personally and academically with greater nuance and openness.

Love,

Eden

LETTER NO. 13 — CREATIVE, PSYCHOTIC AND MYSTIC ENCOUNTERS

Dear Eden,

Thank you for your appreciation and inspiration. You are very generous with your compliments.

In one of my previous letters I talked about people who belong to the Creative Minority and have non-traditional philosophies, personalities and lifestyles. When I studied their biographies, I found out that alongside their creative encounters, some of them also had psychotic and mystic encounters. So, I tried to understand the similarities and differences in those encounters. I want to share those observations and readings with you. I have given a number of references at the end of my letter, in case you want to read any of those books. I look forward to reading your comments. Looking forward to seeing you Saturday evening for dinner and dialogue.

Affectionately,
Gruncle Sohail

....

CREATIVE, PSYCHOTIC AND MYSTIC ENCOUNTERS

INTRODUCTION

How are creative people different from traditional people?

Are creative people like poets, writers and artists more vulnerable to have a nervous breakdown?

Is there an intimate relationship between creativity and insanity?

Why do mentally ill people hear voices of gods, angels and spirits?

How do we differentiate between psychotics and mystics?

Is there a mysterious relationship between creativity, insanity and spirituality?

These are some of the questions I have been trying to answer all of my adult life and to answer those questions I have been studying artists, psychotics and mystics with keen interest. I am quite fascinated by their unique and extraordinary life experiences. I believe these three groups of people have intimate encounters with creativity, spirituality and insanity that transform not only their personalities but also their lifestyles and those of their families and communities.

To have a better understanding of their personalities and develop a greater insight into their lifestyles I interviewed dozens of poets and artists, read the biographies of numerous saints and mystics and treated a large number of schizophrenics and manic-depressives in psychiatric hospitals especially those who had creative potential and experienced auditory hallucinations with religious and spiritual contents. Now that I look back on all those interactions, studies and interviews I am fascinated with the observation that in spite of their obvious differences they had some significant similarities. All of them had unconventional thinking and non-traditional lifestyles. Because they were different from most of the people around them they were judged by others sometimes positively and other times negatively. At times those differences became a blessing while at other times they became a curse. Some poets and mystics were loved and adored while others were penalized and persecuted. Some mentally ill people were treated with compassion while others were ridiculed and ostracized.

CREATIVE, PSYCHOTIC AND MYSTIC ENCOUNTERS

As I followed my passion to have a better understanding of the lives of those extraordinary people, it was important for me to hear about creative, mystic and psychotic encounters directly from those people who experienced them before I read any theoretical formulations about those experiences. I always valued experiences more than analyses. So I started my journey by approaching poets, short story writers and novelists from the East who have been living in the West and had been quite successful in their writing careers. They were quite well respected in the Asian communities in Pakistan, India, Europe and North America. I chose twelve writers and then traveled to different cities in Canada, USA and Europe to interview them in detail discussing not only their creative and immigrant experiences but also how those experiences affected their personalities and lifestyles. I was quite pleased by the enthusiastic response I received.

CREATIVE ENCOUNTERS

During my interviews while I was listening to different poets, I realized that for most of them their creative encounters were a source of joy, excitement, and jubilation. It was a good omen. It meant that their muses were alive and well, healthy, and productive. Experiencing those moments of creativity and giving birth to a poem was quite remarkable. Some could feel the aura and hear an echo in their minds, hearts and souls. Some felt restless, even irritated. It was like experiencing creative labour pains and then the poem was delivered. They had to take some time off from their day-to-day activities to write down the poem. For some when the labour pains began, they often delivered twins or triplets, producing two or three poems at one time.

For some poets the whole experience was unannounced. It was like precipitate labour. They had no advance warning.

In the following pages I am going to present some parts of my interviews with Ashfaq Hussain and Iftikhar Arif, two well respected Urdu poets and then share my impressions about those interviews.

When I asked Ashfaq Hussain if he remembered the day and the circumstances when he wrote his famous poem 'A Love Poem For My Son' he said:

"My poem about my son is a very personal one. My son was two or three years old at the time. One day my wife and son had gone out; I was missing him, which inspired me to write that poem. I don't remember the exact details of the event. I don't think I even knew what I was going to write when I picked up my pen and paper. I must have thought of my son, the temporaries of life and the meaning of our existence. All those things which are not obvious in my poem must have been floating in the back of my mind. I am not saying that I consciously wrote that poem about those issues. All I am saying is that I must have contemplated them at one time or another. I must have thought that children grow up, they become teenagers, then young adults, then grow old and die while life goes on. Many people like myself think about those issues, but at that moment when I was missing my son all those feelings and ideas got transformed into a poem. Maybe I was consoling that I myself might not be living one day but that my son might still be alive. I think it did not take me more than twenty minutes to finish the poem. But that is an ordinary thing. I think the angle that makes that poem special is that it also reflects one aspect of the immigrant experience. I think I must have been preoccupied with my cultural heritage at that time. I must have wondered whether we should thrust our heritage onto our children, set them free in the new society, or thirdly, should we try to strike a balance between two cultures. I think all immigrants share similar dilemmas and problems. Sometimes we like our traditions although we admit that some of them are wrong. Those are the traditions of feudal times and the era of slavery. To break the out-dated traditions is a challenge for each immigrant parent. When I was addressing my son I was actually addressing the next generation. It was just expressed in a personal way."

A Love Poem For My Son

With your eyes,
I will see those days
which have yet to come.

With your feet,
I will run very fast
on dream-pathways
which are still obscure.

With your hands,
I will touch those mountains
whose very thought
makes me breathless.

Those mountains and those roads
on which you walk
a new era
this is yours.

I will not even see
this new era
but my eyes will kiss
its every moment,
with these bright eyes.

In your eyes
like light I shine
like love I abide
like a dream I am alive
in your beautiful eyes
all my dreams
hide in a special corner;
and if perchance these dreams
bloom with fragrance of flowers
in their sweet-scent
you should keep
all the letters of my name
with care.

Translated by: Shehla Burney

When I asked tIfikhar Arif about the nature and experience of the creative process, he said, "different writers and critics have different ways of explaining the creative process. Some people feel satisfied after they finish writing. Others feel happy that they completed a beautiful poem. But in my case, since I have gone through a lot of pain in my life, when I finish a poem I feel sad. I suddenly realize what I am going through. If something is bothering me and making me uncomfortable inside, there is restlessness in me, a lot of tension, a disturbing feeling, so when I write it becomes tangible. It becomes very visible in my poetry.

Let me give you an example. I remember one day I was at a New Year's party in Pakistan. Some of my old friends were there. I had gone to the party alone. Many people stopped and talked to me. As midnight approached, the time when friends and lovers and spouses kissed each other, I noticed that the women around me who were my good friends, started to leave. I was very hurt. I felt uncomfortable, so I asked my driver to take me home. It was hardly a half hour's journey, but in that period I wrote the poem *"Barhavan Khilari"* which translates *"The Twelfth Man"*. When I finished the poem and read it to someone I started crying. I realized that I was the subject of the poem. It turned out to be a very personal poem. For me it was not a catharsis, it was a realization of my unfortunate situation."

The Twelfth Man

In the season of brightness
Countless spectators
Come to spur on
Their favourite teams,
Gather to inspire
Their own idols.

I stand aside
Alienated from it all
Deriding the twelfth player.

How different he is,
That twelfth man!
Amid the game,
The noise,
The roar of acclaim,
He sits alone
And waits -
For the moment to come,
For the time to come,
For that incident to happen
When he too can play
With shouts of praise,
Tumultuous applause,
Words of support
Just for him,
And he'll be one of them
Respected like the rest of them.

But that rarely happens.
People still say
The bond between game and player
Is for life.

From Wonder to Wisdom

But even lifelong bonds can snap,

And the heart that sinks

With the last whistle

Can also break.

And you, Iftikhar,

You too are a twelfth player,

You wait for a moment,

For a time,

For an incident.

You too Iftikhar

Will sink ---

Will break.

Translated by The Poet and Brenda Walker

When I reflected on the interviews I became aware that Ashfaq Hussain and Iftikhar Arif had both delivered their poems in less than half an hour. For them to compose the poem did not take a long time. It seemed as if the Muse came, delivered the creative gift and left.

It was also not a voluntary process for both of them. They were just aware of a feeling, a feeling of missing his son for Ashfaq Hussain and feeling of being lonely in the New Year's party for Iftikhar Arif. Those feelings triggered something in their minds and they connected with their Muse that was residing in the unconscious mind and when a strong feeling in the conscious mind like the fishing rod went deep in the ocean of the unconscious mind, it hooked the poem like a fish and within a short time the fish was brought to the surface. The pen became the fishing rod and the poem was delivered on the shore of the blank page.

It is interesting for me to see that both poems are personal and not personal at the same time. They have multiple layers and like pieces of art can be understood, appreciated and interpreted at multiple levels.

Ashfaq Hussain's poem alongside the personal dilemma also reflects the cultural dilemma of immigrant parents who wonder about the future of their children. Being a positive person rather than being nostalgic and pessimistic, he is optimistic about the future. His poem reflects his faith in his immortality in the form of his son. He offers hope to immigrant parents that their children will go farther and higher in life than their parents and although the first generation of immigrants offer sacrifices, their future generations will receive the rewards and have a more successful life. That poem offers hope to all parents that their children will continue the journey of evolution.

Ashfaq's poem also tries to overcome the fear of death by seeing oneself in one's children. In this way Ashfaq's personal poem also becomes universal and can be enjoyed and appreciated by all human beings.

While Ashfaq's poem is the poem of hope and optimism, Iftikhar Arif's poem is the poem of painful realization. That poem highlights that life is a game and our happiness and success is connected with someone else's tragedy and pain. Our fortune is related to someone else's misfortune. That poem brings to our awareness how human beings are dependent on each other and how for our rise in life we have to wait for someone else's fall. That is the duality of human life, existence and condition. Because of such profound realization Iftikhar Arif's personal poem becomes universal and all human beings from all walks of life and cultures can relate to that.

While Iftikhar Arif's poem makes us feel sad, Ashfaq Hussain's poem also makes us feel optimistic. In this way those poems, those creative gifts of the muse, those creative encounters bring us closer to our deeper and higher selves. They help us get in touch with our dilemmas and dreams. In this way the poets and artists by getting in touch with their unconscious welcome us to get in touch with our own creative side of our mind and personality that I call Creative Self

After interviewing a large number of creative people in my personal life and creative patients in my professional life as a psychotherapist I have come to the understanding that all of us, as human beings have two sides to our personality

A) Traditional Self / Conditioned Self

Traditional Self is the outcome of our familial and cultural conditioning and is guided by *should, must and have to.*

B) Creative Self

Creative Self reflects our true and authentic nature and is guided by *like to, want to and love to.* It is not uncommon for many people to experience conflicts between their Traditional and Creative Self.

Creative people share the Traditional Self with people around them as it reflects the conditioning of the community and the times to which they belong to. Traditional Self helps creative people to have a routine and stability in life. It helps look after the survival issues. On the other hand the Creative Self is personal and unique. Creative Self has a special relationship with the Muse. When the Muse is kind and generous she brings creative gifts in the form of poems or paintings or plays.

Where does this Muse reside?

Many psychologists believe she resides in the unconscious mind and lives in the right side of the brain. While the left side of the brain which is logical and rational and objective helps us live day to day life, the right side of the brain is busy developing the Creative Self and expresses itself in the form of dreams in common people and in the form of pieces of art in creative people.

For Creative people the creative encounter is expressed in the form of creative products.

Sometimes when the creative people read their own poems or see their own paintings or watch their own plays they are surprised as if someone else gave birth to them.

It seems as if there is an interesting and mysterious relationship between Traditional and Creative Self in creative people. For some people Creative Self only expresses occasionally while for others the Muse visits frequently bringing creative gifts to the Traditional Self.

....

CREATIVE AND PSYCHOTIC ENCOUNTERS

A number of years ago I attended an international conference in Brazil to present a paper on Psychotherapy with Immigrants. After presenting my own paper I attended a number of other workshops, seminars and lectures in the conference. One of the presenters was a team from Iceland who had studied the families of people suffering from mental illness. Their conclusions were that the number of creative people including writers, artists, scholars and intellectuals in the families of people suffering from mental illness were two to three times more than the general population. I was quite impressed by their findings. Their results helped me understand not only my own family but also the families of many of my patients. Those research workers wondered whether insanity and creativity were inherited through the same gene.

Since then in my clinical practice I have tried to identify those patients suffering from schizophrenia, bipolar affective disorder and depressions who have creative potential and have never been able to express it consistently and successfully.

While I am writing this I am remembering one of my patients Maureen who had been suffering from depression for a couple of years before she saw me. She had seen a number of doctors and psychiatrists and treated with a wide range of antidepressants but her depression had not responded. After getting her history and seeing her a few times in therapy I realized that she was an accomplished artist as a young woman. She used to teach painting but after her marriage and being involved in family responsibilities she had let her art go in the background. Now that her family responsibilities were over and her husband had left her unexpectedly, she had been feeling depressed.

When I saw a connection between her depression and her creativity, I encouraged her to start painting again. In the beginning she was reluctant but on my insisting she took out her brushes and paints and easels. I asked her to sit in front of a blank canvas for half an hour twice a week. The first six weeks she kept on waiting for her Muse to come back. But after six weeks the Muse got enticed and seduced and she was rewarded for her patience. She started painting and in the next couple of years that she was alive she created more than a couple of dozen paintings and sold each one of them for more than 300 dollars. One day I found her staring at me. When I asked the reason she told me that she was making my portrait and was staring at my eyes as she wanted to paint them perfectly. After a couple of weeks she presented me with a wonderful portrait acknowledging my help to re-introduce her to her Muse. Maureen has passed away but her painting still hangs in my living room, reminding me of the intimate connection between creativity and insanity and possibility of re-connecting with one's Muse even after a break of years or even decades.

MYSTIC ENCOUNTERS

While I was interviewing writers and artists and creative encounters, I was also curious about the lives of sadhus and saints and studied about their mystic encounters. So I decided to read their biographies. During my research I came across two twentieth century who were born in India and during their lifetime claimed to be the rebirth of Buddha. The first one was Dr. Honda, a professor at University of Toronto, who named himself Maitreya after his spiritual enlightenment and called his book of revelations The Gospel of Peace. He shares how the book of revelations is different than the book of poetry by stating;

The birth of every scripture seems to be tied with, and is a product of, spiritual re-birthing of the individual, of experiencing the state which is known by a variety of names, as I said in the beginning: the nirvanic state, enlightenment, satori, self-realization, un-ul-haq, illumination, re-birth, realizing the supra-mental or cosmic consciousness."

As a student of human psychology I was curious how the mystic was similar and different from the poet. I wanted to know how the mystic feels about his extraordinary experience, his unusual encounter and what is his subjective interpretation of his unusual experience. Maitreya shared his experience and interpretation in these words,

" Then, about two months later, around 4.00 in the early hours of the morning I was awakened by the same divine presence, and a voice spoke to me 'take thy pen and write. 'I' shall speak to you about the last book, The Gospel of Peace. Start with the beginning.

There was no beginning. 'I' never created anything. There was no moment of birth, nor shall be one of death; of the universe. Do not be confused and write 'I' never created anything outside and apart from MYSELF..."

There seem to be a number of differences in the encounters of poets and mystics. Poets were in touch with their Creative Self, their unconscious, their Muse, while mystics claimed to experience divine presence and had some communication with gods or angels or spirits when they connected with Mystic Self. For some their God, their creator resided outside the universe, while for others their God resided inside them, deep in their unconscious, as He was present in every part of the universe.

For poets their creativity was part of their humanity while for some mystics their spirituality was part of their divinity.

The other mystic of the twentieth century was J. Krishnamurti. When introduced to Annie Bessant and Charles Leadbeater, members of Theosophical Society in India, they saw spiritual aura surrounding Krishnamurti. Leadbeater was a clergyman well known for his powers of clairvoyance. He claimed that he came in touch with the previous incarnations of Krishnamurti and saw him as a fountain of compassion and wisdom. Annie Bessant took Krishnamurti under her care like a mother and introduced him to the Esoteric Section of the Theosophical Society. She later took Krishnamurti to England for higher levels of spiritual training.

After entering the Esoteric section Krishnamurti's spiritual experiences began. He would enter trance states, have extraordinary visions and then write to Mrs. Bessant, his spiritual guardian. After meditating regularly his mystic encounters became the beginning of his spiritual enlightenment. Some experiences were very painful, traumatic and bizarre. Most people around Krishnamurti were unable to fully understand those experiences but were very supportive of his mysterious journey. They believed that he was experiencing the awakening of his spiritual self, generally known in the spiritual world as *Kundalini* in which the person experiences a transformation of consciousness not accessible to ordinary people.

In one of the letters to Ms. Bessant he wrote about his mystic encounters in these words;

The climax was reached on the 19th. I could not think, nor was I able to do anything, and I was forced by friends here to retire to bed. Then I became almost unconscious, though I was well aware of what was happening around me. I came to myself at about noon each day. On that first day while I was in that state and more conscious of the things around me, I had the first most extraordinary experience. There was a man mending the road; that man was myself; the pickaxe he held was myself; the very stone which he was breaking was a part of me; the tender blade of grass was my very being and the tree beside the man was myself. I almost could feel and think like the roadmen, and I could feel the wind passing through the tree and little ant on the grass I could feel. The birds, the dust and the very noise were a part of me. Just then there was a car passing by at some distance; I was the driver, the engine and the tires, as the car went further away from me, I was going away from myself. I was in everything, or rather everything was in me, inanimate and animate, the mountain, the worm and all breathing things. All day long I remained in this happy condition…I have seen the glorious and helping Light. The fountain of Truth has been revealed to me and the darkness has been dispersed. Love in all its glory has intoxicated my heart; my heart can never be closed. I have drunk at the fountain of joy and eternal Beauty. I am God-intoxicated." (Ref. 1)

For the next few months Krishnamurti continued to have these mystic encounters. During a number of those episodes he became semi-conscious and his friends had to look after him so that he did not hurt himself. Many times he would fall to the floor and experience seizure-like states. On other occasions in his trance, he regressed and talked like a little boy. On one occasion he talked about the death of his mother, revealing that it had really bothered him extensively as a little boy. He recovered from those mystic encounters a transformed man. During one of mystic episode he became convinced that he would lose his mind and become insane.

They know how much a body can stand. If I become a lunatic, look after me…not that I will become a lunatic. They are very careful with the body. I feel so old. Only a bit of me is functioning. I am like an Indian rubber toy, which a child plays with. It is the child that gives it life. *(Ref. 1)*

When I read Krishnamurti's description as a psychiatrist I have no doubt in my mind that he had visual and auditory hallucinations, loss of ego boundaries which are symptoms of mental illness and symptoms of out of body experience and seizure-like activities which are indication of temporal lobe epilepsy.

The question is whether Krishnamurti has encounters with spirituality or insanity or with insanity as a stepping-stone towards spirituality on the journey to enlightenment. The question is what a psychiatrist would have done if he would have examined him during those encounters. Would he have left him alone or admitted him to a psychiatric hospital and treated him with shock treatment and antipsychotic medications and then what would those medications done to him from a psychological and spiritual point of view? Would they have helped or hindered his personal and existential growth.

While I was reading the biography of Krishnamurti, I came across one of his contemporaries Guru Rajneesh, who was also born in India and had claimed to have achieved spiritual enlightenment. Rajneesh's early phase of spiritual journey had some similarities with that of Krishnamurti. They both had mystic encounters which had features similar to psychotic encounters. Rajneesh's biographer James Gordon describes his transformation as a young adult in these words;

Soon he seemed more basket case than beatnik. He continued to challenge the received ideas of his friends and teachers, but his precocious self-assurance disintegrated. He felt alone and insecure. He suffered from disabling headaches. "For one year" he recalled 'it was almost impossible to know what was happening...Just to keep myself alive was a very difficult thing, because all appetite disappeared. I could not talk to anybody. In every other sentence I would forget what I was saying.'

He said he ran up to sixteen miles a day ' just to feel myself' and spent days at a time lying on the floor of his room counting from one to one hundred and back again. He sat in high trees to meditate. Once, he reported, his body fell to the ground but his 'consciousness' stayed in the air, connected by a glittering silver cord to his navel. He felt the 'connection...between his physical body and the spiritual being...disintegrate." During this year his hair and beard were wild, his eyes prettier-naturally bright.

Rajneesh had the sense he was going through an extremely important change. His concerned parents believed he was going crazy. They took their son to one physician after another. In the West, indeed in modern India, there would have been little doubt about Rajneesh's condition. To most observers the situation would have looked less like an ordinary adolescent identity crisis and more like an incipient psychotic episode. Doctors would probably have hospitalized him, tranquilizers might have been prescribed.

As it happened, Rajneesh was seen by a Vaidiya, a traditional Ayurvedic physician, who construed his symptoms differently. The Vaidiya believed that the symptoms were those of divine intoxication, that the apparent breakdown was actually a kind of breakthrough. Rajneesh, the Vaidiya said, was 'reaching home'.

Rajneesh said that on March 21st, 1953, at the age of twenty-one, he did 'reach home'. He became enlightened...'a new energy' 'a new freedom came'...'There was no gravitation' he said years later, ' I was feeling weightless…For the first time the drop had fallen into the ocean…I was the ocean…The moment I entered the garden everything became luminous…alive…beautiful". He sat under a Maulshree tree. There was no time, and 'the whole universe…luminous, throbbing, became a benediction.' (Ref. 2. p 25)

PSYCHOTIC ENCOUNTERS

As a psychiatrist one of the fundamental questions is:

How can the mystic encounters be separated from the psychotic encounters of schizophrenics? Who needs treatment and medications and who does not? While I was reading the experiences of Krishnamurti and Rajneesh I was thinking about one of my young patients who suffered from schizophrenia and used to be preoccupied by religious and spiritual matters and as his condition deteriorated his life started to disintegrate. He had very poor self-esteem. He believed he was ugly and nobody liked him. Unfortunately his condition did not respond to medications, psychotherapy or even hospitalization.

One day he showed me one of his poems, which read

HERE AT HOME

Come inside my name in hell
Let me give you pain and agony so you won't feel well
Over in the distance across the flames of darkness you can hear a bell

I welcome you into my fear I see you like it I can tell

Up from God in heaven above I was defeated and fell

Down to the stinking creating God made

I sit here down on earth a demon of hade

I hate man's soul and make him to fade

Into the night the dark gloom and shade

Death destruction is my name and confusion and death on earth all of

it will I claim

The war pains grace in man's head---take a look around and know my

name

The name of satan is of hell, fury furnace, reign

God is but a dove, yet I am the dragon

and crush his weak wings all over each I claim suffering and life,

love of greed I sing

I love the danger of battle the screams of man in my

ear I love to hear it ring

Against spikes and stakes---God's people will I crush and fling

Come into me satan and darken my soul

Down here in my hell inside my home. (Ref. 3)

This young schizophrenic was so tormented by his psychotic encounters that after a few months of writing that poem he committed suicide.

Silvano Arieti, a famous American psychiatrist, comments on the differences between psychotic and mystic encounters.

'Mystical experiences seem to correspond to what are called hallucinations and delusions in psychiatric terms---it is easy to confuse religious mystics with psychotic patients especially those psychotics who have hallucinations and delusions with a religious content

Arieti feels that there are marked differences between them. He writes,

The individual who experiences them [mystic encounters] has a marked rise in self-esteem and a sense of his being or becoming a worthwhile and very active person. He has been given a mission, a special insight, and from now on he must be on the move doing something important---more important than his life.

In mystical experiences we have a tradition of auto-hypnosis. A subject puts himself into a state of a trance and projects power to the divinity---the hypnosis is time limited and totally reversible.

The hallucinatory and delusional experiences of the schizophrenic are generally accompanied by a more or less apparent disintegration of the whole person. Religious and mystical experiences seem to result in a strengthening and enriching of the personality. (Ref. 4)

John White, editor of a book *What is Enlightenment?*, believes that a nervous breakdown with auditory hallucinations, loss of ego boundaries, paranoia and other symptoms of mental illness might be a transitory step towards a breakthrough. Those people who cannot go to the next stage become mentally ill while those who are lucky to have a strong personality, supportive friends or an experienced spiritual teacher might be guided to the next stage of mystic development and achieve nirvana and enlightenment. He believes that the journey of spiritual enlightenment can go through three stages: *'from arthonoia through paranoia to metanoia. We grow from arthonoia – that is, the common, every day state of ego centered mind – to metanoia only by going through paranoia, a state in which the mind is deranged with (that is, taken apart) and rearranged through spiritual discipline so that clear perception of reality might be experienced. Conventional western psychologists regard paranoia as a pathological breakdown. It often is, of course, but seen from this perspective, it is not necessarily so. Rather, it can be a breakthrough – not the final breakthrough, to be sure, but a necessary stage of development on the way to realization of the kingdom'.*

Paranoia is a condition well understood by mystical and sacred traditions. The spiritual disciplines that people practice under the guidance of guru or master are designed to ease and quicken the passage through paranoia so that the practitioner doesn't get lost in the labyrinth of inner space and become a casualty.

Because metanoia has by large not been experienced by the founders of western psychology and psychotherapy, paranoia has not felt fully understood in our culture. It is seen as an aberrant dead end rather than a necessary precondition to higher consciousness. It is not understood that the confusion, discomfort, and suffering experienced in paranoia are due entirely to the destruction of an illusion, ego. The less we cling to that illusion, the less we suffer." *(Ref. 5, p 120)*

It is interesting to note that neither do all psychotics have mystic encounters nor do all mystics experience a psychotic breakdown.

Krishnamurti after experiencing mystic encounters developed a mystic personality and defined a new role in his life. In Feb 1927 he wrote to Leadbeater

I know my destiny and my work. I know with certainty that I am blending into the consciousness of the one Teacher and that he will completely fill me. I feel and I know also that my cup is nearly full to the brim and that it will overflow soon. Till then I must abide quietly and with eager patience. I long to make and will make everybody happy.

In April 1927, Mrs. Bessant said to the Associated Press in the United States, "The Divine Spirit has descended once more on a man Krishnamurti, who in his lifetime is literally perfect as those who know him can testify. The World Teacher is here." Mrs Bessant's life-long dream had come true. Her spiritual student had finally graduated.

After Krishnamurti started a new road towards enlightenment, his first step was to denounce all traditions, all cults, all religious institutions, all teachers, all centers of authority including his own Theosophical Society. In August 1929 he announced his resignation from the Society in the presence of Mrs. Bessant and started his solitary journey. Describing his vision for the future he said

The vision is total to me that is liberation *(Ref. 1, p 104)*

After that announcement and for the rest of his life, his teachings were based on his philosophy which he stated as,

I maintain that Truth is a pathless land, and you cannot approach it by any other path whatsoever, by any religion, by any sect...Truth being limitless, unconditioned, unapproachable by any path whatsoever, cannot be organized, nor should any organization be formed to lead or to coerce people along any particular path (Ref. 1 p 104)

After his resignation, his teacher Mrs. Bessant expressed a desire to resign from the Society and become his disciple but Krishnamurti refused to accept anyone as his disciple, even the very loyal and dedicated Mrs. Bessant.

Krishnamurti, for the next half a century, travelled around the world giving lectures, meeting people from all walks of life sharing his knowledge, experience and wisdom. Those who consulted him for their problems included three generations of prime ministers of India, Jawarlal Nehru, his daughter Indira Gandhi and her son Rajiv Gandhi. People who admired his knowledge and wisdom included the Dalai Lama, Bernard Shaw, Aldous Huxley, Henry Miller, R.D. Laing, Joseph Campbell and many -more.

On the other hand Rajneesh became quite notorious and was known as the sex-guru and pseudo-mystic.

Rajneesh had to leave India and established a commune in America. For a while he was so successful that he had accumulated, among other trappings of wealth, a fleet of 99 Rolls Royces. However, he got into legal difficulties with the local community and was asked to leave the country. Unfortunately his motherland refused to take him so for a few years he wandered around in different parts of the world until his death in 1990, 'allegedly as a result of either poisoning or from full blown AIDS' *(Ref 1, p 65)*. In the years since his death, millions of people have visited his Ashram in India. Interestingly the leader of the movement is a Canadian by the name of Swami Mike, son of a British Columbia judge.

According to one report, the average revenue generated in that Ashram in Poona, India is nearly 50 million dollars a year.

....

THE ROLE OF TEMPORAL LOBES IN CREATIVE, PSYCHOTIC AND MYSTIC ENCOUNTERS

While I was contemplating about the similarities between creative encounters of a poet, psychotic encounters of a schizophrenic and mystic encounters of a saint and wondering as a secular humanist whether the creative gift of the Muse, and the voices of God and Satan have the same origin, our own unconscious, I remembered a number of my patients that I looked after in the last twenty years of my clinical practice who suffered from temporal lobe epilepsy. Before they were properly diagnosed they had seen numerous doctors and visited different clinics and hospitals and were treated with a wide range of antipsychotics, antidepressants and anxiolytics with no beneficial effect. Those patients had been a mystery for their families, friends and physicians alike. They could be divided in two groups:

A) The first group experienced auditory hallucinations, delusions, thought disorder and loss of ego boundaries. The content of symptoms was persecutory. They were diagnosed as schizophrenics and treated with antipsychotics but unlike other schizophrenics these symptoms seemed to appear and disappear mysteriously unrelated to taking medications.

B) The second group had a religious and spiritual flavour to their psychotic symptoms. They heard voices of God and believed they had special powers and were the chosen ones to deliver a special message to the world. Their families were quite perturbed by the whole experience. They were unsure whether their relatives were saints or psychotics. Patients believed they were having a spiritual breakthrough while the families believed they were having a nervous breakdown.

Interestingly after EEGs were done and these patients were diagnosed as suffering from temporal lobe epilepsy and treated with antiepileptics like Tegratol, those symptoms came in control and those patients started leading healthy, happy and stable lives. Later on they felt embarrassed talking about their psychotic and mystic encounters. One of them called them 'disturbing and confusing nightmares'.

When I met those patients and heard their stories from them and their families I wondered about the role of temporal lobes in the dynamics of creative, psychotic and mystic encounters. And then I came across Dr. Robert Buckman's book *Can We Be Good Without God*. In that book he presents an enlightening review of the literature and research done by a number of neurologists. He brings to our attention that Temporal Lobes play a significant role in all those perceptions and experiences that we associate with creative, psychotic and mystic encounters. He shares the activities of right and left temporal lobes in these words, '*The left temporal lobe functions as a major component of your language skills and (depending on the part of it we are talking about) some aspects of your motor skills. Damage in this area (for example from a stroke or a head injury) usually produces major difficulties with speech (as with aphasia or dysphasia) or certain types of difficulties in moving or doing things (sometimes called a dyspraxia)...temporal lobe on the right side of your brain... [has] something to do with the person's perception of reality and of himself or herself...problems in the right temporal lobe produce disturbances of perception and experiences."(Ref 6, p 115)*. Many of these changes are proven by the EEG [electroencephalographic] invented in 1940s and since used in studying epileptic patients and sleep problems in normal people.

Based on EEG studies Buckman highlights that human beings can be divided in three groups depending upon the sensitivity of temporal lobes.

Those people who have highly sensitive temporal lobes suffer from temporal lobe epilepsy as they have spontaneous firing of the neurons of the temporal lobe. Dr. Hughlings Jackson studied those epileptics and discovered that their auras, hallucinations and out of body experiences were not much different than what was reported by saints in their mystic encounters. During those epileptic seizures the auras '...*include some very particular sensations and experiences. These may include any (or several) of the following: auditory hallucinations (hearing voices), déjà vu (the feeling of seeing something before), visual hallucinations, experiencing funny smells, a feeling of particular peace, a sensation of deep understanding or of profound and significant knowledge and a feeling of being outside one's body.'(Ref 6, p 119)*

One such example was Fyodor Dostoessky, a famous Russian writer, who suffered from temporal lobe epilepsy and shared his experiences in these words,

"*All of the forces of life gathered convulsively all at once to the highest attainable consciousness. The sensation of life, of being, multiplied tenfold at that moment, all passion, all doubts, all unrests, were resolved as in a higher peace, then a peace full of...harmonious joy and hope. And then a scene suddenly as if something was opening up in the soul: an indescribable, an unknown light radiated, by which the ultimate essence of things was made visible and recognizable. All this lasted at most a second.* (Ref 6, p 120)

Based on the experiences of temporal lobe epileptics some neurologists wonder whether many saints and mystics like Joan of Arc suffered from Temporal Lobe Epilepsy.

Dr. Wilder Penfield, the Canadian neurosurgeon "mapped out the functions of the various areas of the brain" and discovered "When *he stimulated the motor areas, patients experienced involuntary movements or twitches of the arm or leg or lips or some other part of the body. But when he stimulated the temporal lobe on the right side, there was no movement of any part of the body. Instead, the patients reported a wide variety of significant experiences, perceptions and/or feelings. The phenomena reported were basically the same as the auras accompanying temporal lobe seizures--- feelings of great peace, of deep understanding, of consciousness of another being, of sensations of taste, sight or sound and so on.' (Ref 6, p 122)*

Those people who have temporal lobes more sensitive than average but less sensitive than epileptics have creative encounters and become poets and artists and actors as it is easy for them to enter imaginary worlds and create characters or play roles of other people.

'...drama, poetry and other creative acts: activities that require the person to 'get into' another world or another mode are associated with high temporal lobe scores.' (Ref. 6, p 133)

Even those people who have average temporal lobes and do not suffer from temporal lobe epilepsy and are not poets or actors, when their temporal lobes are stimulated by electrodes in the laboratory they have similar experiences. Rather than having epileptic fits they have perceptual and sensory experiences similar to the ones shared by the mystics. When M.A. Persinger did experiments on volunteers by stimulating their temporal lobes he noticed, *"...Sometimes the sensations were visual or auditory, sometimes they were complex experiences, sometimes they were based on actual memories; sometimes they were fundamental and deep-rooted feelings. Many of them, however, had to do with a feeling of peace, of serenity, of being one with nature and often of being in the presence of another consciousness (another being). Some people felt that they were near the presence of aliens. Others experienced deeply spiritual or religious feelings. Some reported that they were in the presence of god, and some heard his voice."* (Ref 6, p 125)

How do we understand all those similarities? Julian Jaynes tried to explain those encounters based on his theory of Right/Left Brain functioning. He believes that the Temporal Lobe of the Left Brain deals with language while the Temporal Lobe of the Right Brain deals with sensory, perceptual and aesthetic experiences. He believes that psychotic, creative and mystic experiences originate in the Right Brain and when messages are sent to the Left Brain, the Left Brain does not own it and feels as if those messages came from the outside and depending upon the personality and philosophy of the person and the culture interpreted in different ways. Buckman explains, *" In 1962, a scientist, historian and thinker named Julian Jaynes popularized the idea that our minds all work in a 'right-brain / left-*

brain' manner...In *Origins of Consciousness in the Breakdown of the Bi-cameral Mind* Jaynes comes to some startling conclusions.

He suggests that consciousness---awareness of one's self as a person and personality---did not evolve steadily or even early in the human mind's history. Jaynes suggests that what we nowadays regard as 'our own thoughts' were originally perceived by the thinker as voices coming from the spirits of dead ancestors. Jaynes proposed that thoughts originating in the right side of the brain crossed over into the left, where they were not recognized as the person's own but seemed to arrive from outside." Dr. Robert Buckman concludes his discussion by stating his opinion *"If the limbic system [that includes temporal lobes] is activated by means of the temporal lobe, a person will have an experience of the spiritual or divine type. God is--- literally--- a state of mind." (Ref 7, p 144)*

After reviewing the literature and life stories of people it seems to be as if there are a number of creative, psychotic and mystic encounters that human beings from all walks of life and cultures experience but the interpretation of those experiences depend upon the belief structures of those people who experience them and the families and cultures they belong to. Secular people, families and cultures associate them with their own brains and unconscious minds and associate the voices with the gifts of Muse.

Spiritual people, families and cultures associate the same experiences with spirits, angels or God residing in their own unconscious.

Religious people, families and cultures explain the same experiences by associating them with the traditional concept of God and the Creator who is outside the universe and sends messages to specially chosen people who are recognized as saints and mystics and prophets by their communities.

As a psychotherapist and a secular humanist I believe that those extraordinary experiences are part of our humanity while associating them with God and divinity is part of mythology that we have culturally inherited over the centuries. As a psychiatrist I believe that it is important for us in our personal and professional lives to identify

A) Those artists and mystics who do not experience emotional problems and suffer from nervous breakdowns

B) Those patients who suffer from temporal lobe epilepsy, bipolar disorder and schizophrenia and offer them the best treatment we can offer to decrease their suffering

C) Those people who want to follow the creative and mystic paths and develop their creative and mystic self and are going through a psychotic state as a part of the journey. It might be better to offer them support and encouragement rather than offer them traditional psychiatric treatment and give them antipsychotics. But it would be important to follow them for a while to see whether their personalities are strengthened or weakened by those extraordinary experiences.

D) Those people who need psychotherapy to encourage their mystic and creative potential as they suffer because they have not been able to express their creativity and get in touch with their spirituality.

I believe time has come for poets, psychologists, priests, mystics and psychotherapists to work together so that they can serve humanity to the best of their abilities by understanding the personalities of artists, psychotics and mystics and then helping them become the best they can and share their creative gifts with their families and communities. I believe that those gifts belong to the whole of humanity.

References

1. Jayakar Papul *Krishnamurti- A Biography* Harper and Rowe Publishers, New York USA 1986

2. Gordon James *Golden Guru* Stephen Green Press USA 2000

3. Sohail Khalid *Schizophrenia* Creative Links Canada 1990

4. Arieti Silvana *Creativity : The Magic Synthesis* Basic Books Inc. USA 1976

5. John White *What is Enlightenment* Paragon Press New York USA 1995

6. Buckman Robert *Can we be good without God* Penguin Books New York USA 2000

7. Jaynes Julian *The Origin of Consciousness in the breakdown of the Bicameral Mind* Mariner Books New York USA 1997

LETTER NO. 14 — CREATIVITY AND MENTAL ILLNESS

Dear Gruncle Sohail,

Thank you for your thoughtful letter. I was particularly struck by your mention of the genetic connection between creativity and insanity. The idea that there might be a shared biological or psychological undercurrent is both compelling and unsettling, which inspired me to write my own article on the subject. I would love to hear your thoughts on this, as it ties in so closely with the ideas you've been exploring. I'm looking forward to discussing this further over dinner on Thursday.

The relationship between creativity and mental health has long intrigued both researchers and the public, often evoking the archetype of the "tortured artist" or the "mad genius." Over time, empirical studies have suggested a compelling association between creative professions and the incidence of mood disorders, particularly bipolar disorder and schizophrenia. While the connection between creativity and mental illness is widely acknowledged, the underlying factors that drive this association remain complex and multifaceted. Advancements in genomics and psychological research are gradually unraveling the genetic and cognitive traits that may explain why individuals with exceptional creative abilities are often more susceptible to mental health challenges. This essay explores the genetic overlap between creativity and psychiatric conditions, examining how shared traits may both foster artistic brilliance and predispose individuals to emotional instability.

Empirical studies have consistently indicated a higher incidence of mood disorders, particularly bipolar disorder, among individuals in creative professions such as writers, artists, and musicians. A landmark 2012 study by researchers at the Karolinska Institute in Sweden found that people in creative fields were more likely to have a close relative diagnosed with schizophrenia, bipolar disorder, or autism spectrum disorders. This observation suggests not only a correlation but also a potential shared genetic underpinning.

Modern genomics has provided tools to examine the genetic architecture behind both creativity and psychiatric conditions. Genome-wide association studies (GWAS) have identified certain genes and gene variants associated with an increased risk of mental illnesses like schizophrenia and bipolar disorder. Interestingly, some of these same variants appear to be more common in individuals with high levels of creativity. For example, genes that regulate dopamine, a neurotransmitter involved in cognitive flexibility and susceptibility to psychosis, have been implicated. A 2015 study published in Nature

Neuroscience found that individuals with high polygenic risk scores for schizophrenia and bipolar disorder were more likely to be engaged in creative professions.

These findings suggest a genetic overlap, but not a deterministic cause-and-effect relationship. Rather, certain genetic traits may predispose individuals both to creative thinking and to vulnerabilities for mental health disorders. The genetic traits linked to both creativity and mental illness is complex and polygenic, meaning they are influenced by numerous genes rather than a single one. Each gene contributes only a small amount to the overall risk or propensity. These traits are heritable, meaning they can be passed down from parent to child, but they are also shaped by environmental and developmental factors.

For instance, a child who inherits a heightened sensitivity to emotional stimuli is likely to experience the world with intense emotional depth and reactivity. This sensitivity can be a powerful asset in artistic or creative domains, where the ability to perceive subtle emotional nuances enables profound expression that resonates with others. Poets, musicians, and visual artists often draw on their own intense inner experiences to create works that move audiences. However, this same sensitivity can become a double-edged sword. When emotions are difficult to regulate or felt too intensely, the individual may be more vulnerable to conditions like anxiety and depression. Emotional hypersensitivity may contribute to rumination, an over-identification with distressing thoughts, and an overwhelming reaction to stress, each of which are risk factors for mood disorders.

Similarly, a child who inherits an enhanced capacity for associative thinking may excel at connecting seemingly unrelated ideas, a hallmark of creative problem-solving and innovation. This type of thinking supports metaphor-making, conceptual blending, and improvisation, all of which are crucial in fields ranging from the arts to science and entrepreneurship. However, in more extreme forms, associative thinking can resemble the cognitive disorganization observed in certain psychiatric conditions, such as schizophrenia. For example, in schizophrenia, "loose associations" can cause thoughts to jump unpredictably from one topic to another, making speech or writing incoherent. While not all highly associative thinkers will develop mental illness, the trait exists on a spectrum, and when combined with other genetic or environmental risk factors, it may increase susceptibility to thought disorders. Thus, what fosters creative brilliance in one context may mirror cognitive dysfunction in another, underscoring the delicate balance between imaginative capacity and mental stability.

It is crucial to note that genetics alone does not determine an individual's fate. Many people with a genetic predisposition to mental illness never develop such conditions, and many highly creative individuals do not experience psychiatric challenges. Genetic predisposition is only one part of the equation. Environment plays a significant role in shaping both creative potential and mental health outcomes. Supportive family dynamics, education, early-life experiences, and access to mental health resources all influence whether a genetically predisposed trait becomes strength or a liability. Furthermore, traits associated with creativity, such as openness to experience, divergent thinking, and emotional depth, can be nurtured or hindered depending on one's environment.

Throughout history, numerous individuals have demonstrated exceptional creativity, often walking a fine line between brilliance and madness. Modern behavioural genetics has begun to untangle this intricate relationship by examining the heritability of traits associated with both creativity, such as divergent thinking, openness to experience, and pattern recognition, and psychiatric conditions like bipolar disorder and schizophrenia.

Twin and family studies suggest that some of the same genetic variants that promote novel ideation and cognitive flexibility may also increase susceptibility to mood swings, psychotic episodes, or other features commonly categorized as "insanity." In this view, creativity and mental illness are not mutually exclusive categories, but overlapping spectra whose shared genetic underpinnings can manifest in diverse ways, depending on other biological, environmental, and developmental factors.

However, possessing a genetic predisposition does not guarantee that an individual will evolve into a tortured artist or a manic polymath; it merely raises the probability, much like a loaded, but not firing, gun. Many creative geniuses exhibit remarkable resilience, channeling intense emotional experiences into art, literature, or scientific discovery without succumbing to debilitating illness. Conversely, those with psychiatric diagnoses may lack creative outlets or supportive networks that would allow them to harness their unique perspectives constructively. The distinction, therefore, lies not solely in genes, but in how those genetic risks are expressed, moderated by social environment, personal coping strategies, and access to mental health resources. It is at this intersection that we begin to see how extremes of thought and feeling can fuel both inspired creative leaps and, in some cases, life-threatening disorders.

The "Mad Genius Paradox" encapsulates this dynamic: the puzzling observation that the very qualities that drive extraordinary creative achievement also appear to predispose individuals to serious mental health challenges. At first glance, this seems counterintuitive: if certain gene variants impair emotional regulation or cognitive stability, why would they persist through natural selection? One theory posits that mild expressions of these variants confer adaptive benefits like heightened alertness, associative thinking, and risk-taking,that historically increased survival or reproductive success. In contrast, only the rare, extreme manifestations tip into pathology. As a result, populations retain these alleles, as the average payoff, in terms of innovation and problem-solving, outweighs the occasional cost of severe disorder.

The paradox within the "Mad Genius Paradox" lies in the tension between dysfunction and brilliance. Mental illnesses such as bipolar disorder, schizophrenia, and depression are generally disabling, causing significant distress and impairing daily functioning. Creativity, on the other hand, requires cognitive flexibility, persistence, and novelty, traits seemingly at odds with the debilitating aspects of mental illness. How, then, can these opposites coexist, and even fuel each other?

The answer lies in nuance. Modern psychological research suggests that creativity and psychopathology may be linked, not directly or universally, but through shared traits, genetic overlaps, and specific cognitive processes that, when moderated, support creative thinking.

A growing body of research indicates that highly creative individuals are more likely to experience certain mental health disorders, particularly mood disorders. However, this trend is not uniform across all creative fields. Notably, the association is strongest in artistic domains, such as writing, visual arts, and music, while scientific and technical creativity appears less linked to mental illness.

Kay Redfield Jamison, a clinical psychologist and professor of psychiatry at Johns Hopkins University, is a leading authority on mood disorders. In her influential book *Touched with Fire* (1993), she examined the relationship between bipolar disorder and artistic creativity. Drawing from both clinical data and her personal experience with bipolar disorder, Jamison argued that the elevated mood states associated with the illness can enhance productivity, energy, and originality in artists and writers, highlighting the complex interplay between mental illness and creative drive.

Nancy Andreasen, a prominent neuroscientist and psychiatrist, conducted a 1987 study of highly accomplished writers, revealing that 80% had experienced mood disorders, compared to just 30% in a control group. Additionally, mental illness was more prevalent among the writers' first-degree relatives, suggesting a possible genetic or familial influence.

Simon Kyaga, a Swedish psychiatrist and researcher at the Karolinska Institute, led one of the largest population-based studies on this topic. His team analyzed data from over one million individuals in Sweden and found that people in creative professions, particularly writers, artists, and musicians, were more likely to be diagnosed with mood disorders, schizophrenia, and anxiety. However, no such correlation was found among creative scientists and engineers, lending empirical support to the notion that the creativity-psychopathology link is domain-specific.

Rather than implying a direct cause-and-effect relationship, researchers increasingly propose that creativity and psychopathology may both arise from shared underlying psychological traits. These traits, when present in milder forms, can contribute positively to creative thought, while in more extreme manifestations, they may be associated with mental illness. This perspective allows for a more nuanced understanding of the often-observed link between creative achievement and psychological vulnerability, emphasizing a continuum rather than a binary.

One such trait is divergent thinking, the ability to generate multiple novel ideas from a single prompt. This cognitive flexibility is a hallmark of creativity and has been linked to cognitive disinhibition, a tendency to allow more information into conscious awareness. Interestingly, cognitive disinhibition is also present in certain forms of psychosis, suggesting a shared cognitive architecture.

The complex relationship between creativity and mental health reveals an intricate interplay of genetic predispositions, cognitive traits, and environmental influences. Empirical studies suggest a notable association between creative professions and mood disorders, particularly bipolar-disorder and schizophrenia, but this connection is far from deterministic. Instead, it reflects a nuanced spectrum, where shared genetic traits can both drive extraordinary creative abilities and increase susceptibility to mental illness. Traits such as heightened emotional sensitivity and cognitive flexibility may enhance artistic brilliance, yet they also leave individuals vulnerable to emotional instability. Ultimately, creativity and mental illness are not opposing forces but overlapping phenomena, shaped by the balance between genetic factors, life experiences, and social context. As research advances, a deeper understanding of the genetic and cognitive foundations behind both creativity and psychopathology will help illuminate how genius and mental health are intertwined, opening new paths for support, intervention, and expression.

Sincerely,

Eden

LETTER NO. 15 — FOUR TRADITIONS

Dear Eden,

The more I read your letters the more I get impressed. I find it hard to believe that you are so wise and insightful at such a young age. You are a 16 year old girl but you think like a 60 year old professor.

In your letter you highlighted different connections between creativity and insanity. When I found out about that connection I started reading biographies of those creative personalities who suffered from depression or bipolar disorder or schizophrenia committed suicide. I have written a number of blogs about dilemmas and dreams, struggles and successes of Virginia Woolf, Sylvia Plath, Ernest Hemmingway and Vincent Van Gogh.

You might be interested to know that in psychiatry we have a diagnosis called Van Gogh Syndrome. It is a diagnosis given to those people who, because of their mental illness, cut an organ of their body because Van Gogh had cut his ear in one of his psychotic breakdowns. That is why in some of self-portraits he has covered one of his ears in his paintings.

Dear Eden,

So far in my letters, I have been focusing on the human psyche of one person. It is a microscopic study on humanity. Now I want to move to the telescopic study of humanity that includes human sociology, history and philosophy. Being a humanist, who believes in biological, psychological, social and cultural evolution, when I studied human history I found out that there are four traditions that human beings have created over the centuries. Let me share some of the highlights of those traditions with you. I hope you enjoy them.

Peacefully,
Gruncle Sohail

THE EVOLUTION OF HUMAN CONSCIOUSNESS

FOUR TRADITIONS

When we reflect on human history and study the evolution of human consciousness, we become aware that throughout history in different communities, countries and cultures, a variety of traditions were created and practised. There were leaders and followers, there were scholars and philosophers, and there were students and disciples. Rather than going into a detailed academic discussion, I would like to capture the essence of the collective wisdom of the centuries by dividing them into four cultural and philosophical traditions.

The first tradition was the Humanist Tradition. It was presented by Confucius and Lao Tzu in China. Both of these scholars and philosophers presented their ideas and ideals to inspire people to become better human beings individually and collectively. Confucius presented the Golden Rule to humanity and suggested that we need to treat others the way we would like to be treated by them. The Golden Rule became the basis of a caring and compassionate humanist philosophy. Lao Tzu suggested that to lead a simple and meaningful life we need to stay close to nature. He believed that nature's way was Tao and the closer we stay to our own nature and the nature of our environment, the easier it will be for us to lead a healthy, happy and peaceful life.

It is interesting to note that Confucius and Lao Tzu did not mention the concepts of God, prophets, life after death, heaven or hell in their philosophy. They believed that we did not need divine revelations to become better human beings and create just and peaceful communities.

The second tradition was the Spiritual Tradition. It was presented by Buddha and Mahavira in India. They believed that human attachment to people and possessions is the main source of suffering. Buddha and Mahavira encouraged their followers to learn to meditate and emotionally detach themselves from their environments to find peace. Buddha also believed in a soul separate from the body that kept returning to the earth to purify itself. Once it found enlightenment and nirvana, the soul no longer needed to make this journey.

The third tradition was the Religious Tradition. It was presented by Zarathustra in Iran. Zarathustra presented the ideas of a Heavenly God, Ahura Mazda, the God of Wisdom, divine revelations, sin and virtue, life after death, heaven and hell. Zarathustra believed that if human beings followed divine revelations they would lead a happy and peaceful life on earth and go to heaven in the afterlife.

Zarathustra's ideas and ideals became popular in the Middle East and became part of Abrahamic religious traditions that gave birth to Judaism, Christianity and Islam. Those three monotheistic religions are the off-springs of Zarathustrian ideology. Their followers also believe in a soul separate from the body; but such a soul does not come back to earth like the Buddhist soul, rather it waits for the Day of Judgment to be sent to hell or heaven. Since the followers of Christianity and Islam believed in preaching, their preachers traveled to the four corners of the world to spread the holy message. Some followers of these religions also believed in holy wars--crusades and jihads. Because of those preachers and holy warriors there are billions of followers of Christianity and Islam all over the world.

The fourth tradition was the Philosophical Tradition. It was presented by Greek philosophers like Hippocrates, Socrates, Plato and Aristotle. These philosophers presented the idea that all things and events in life follow the laws of nature and by knowing those laws we can unravel the mysteries of nature.

Hippocrates became the Father of Medicine. He told his patients that rather than praying and fasting and offering sacrifices to Gods for their sins, they should heal their bodies by a balanced diet, a good night's sleep, and regular exercise. He believed that walking was the best exercise. Hippocrates was the first physician who separated medicine from religion.

Socrates, another Greek philosopher, became the Father of Philosophy. He encouraged logical, rational and analytical thinking as he believed that reason was more important than revelation to solve human problems. Socrates inspired young people to question and challenge age-old traditions. Many traditional Greeks did not like the Socratic Method, so they accused him of misguiding the youth and not believing in the Greek gods. As his punishment, Socrates drank a cup of poison and sacrifices his life for his ideals. Socrates did not write down his ideas but his student Plato documented his philosophy in the form of dialogues, because Socrates believed that dialogue, rather than a monologue, was a better way to discover truth. He believed that unexamined life was not worth living.

Plato created an academy to teach philosophy and science that became the prototype of modern Western universities. Plato's student Aristotle made valuable contributions to the world of politics. Greek philosophers offered a road map to create a just and peaceful republic. They also made significant contributions to the disciplines of science and human psychology.

Over the centuries, Greek philosophers were translated and introduced to Europe by Arab philosophers like Al Kindi, Al Farabi, Avicenna and Ibn Rushd. Based on the foundations laid down by Greek philosophers, European scholars built tall buildings of philosophy and science.

In the last three centuries, the significant discoveries of scientists can be broadly classified into four major groups.

Biologists like Charles Darwin,

Psychologists like Sigmund Freud,

Sociologists like Karl Marx and

Cosmologists like Stephen Hawking made revolutionary contributions to the disciplines of biology, psychology, sociology and cosmology.

While scientists were discovering methods to collect evidence and discover the laws of nature, caring and compassionate reformers from different communities and cultures were discovering ways to resolve conflicts gracefully. They presented their secular ideas and humanist ideals and fought for human rights. These philosophers and reformers like Leo Tolstoy, Mohandas Gandhi and Martin Luther King, Jr. inspired their followers to rise above racial, religious, linguistic and gender differences and discover common bonds of humanity. They shared with us that to create a peaceful world we need to cherish our differences and recognize that we are all part of the same family, the human family.

In the contemporary world, peaceful followers of different religious and spiritual, secular and scientific traditions are breaking down walls of ignorance and prejudice and building bridges of caring and compassion, harmony and peace so that we can all grow to the next stage of human evolution and create a peaceful world together. These are our dreams but we need to dream before we can make them realities.

LETTER NO. 16 — FROM ANIMISM TO MONOTHEISM TO PLURALISM

Dear Gruncle Sohail,

I want to start by expressing my sincere appreciation for your thoughtful and insightful perspective on the evolution of human consciousness and the framework of the four traditions. Your analysis provides a compelling lens through which to understand such a complex and profound topic, and it's clear that you have given it considerable depth and nuance. That said, while I deeply respect your interpretation, my own view of the four traditions slightly diverges from the ones you described. In my perspective, the four traditions can be understood as Animism and Spiritual Cosmologies, Monotheism and Universal Religion, Humanism and Enlightenment Rationalism, and finally Digital Individualism and Postmodern Pluralism. I see each of these traditions as playing a pivotal role in shaping human consciousness and societal structures, each emerging during distinct historical epochs. Importantly, they also set the stage for the emergence of the next tradition, creating a dynamic and ongoing evolution of thought, belief, and identity. This framework, I believe, captures both the continuity and the transformation inherent in our collective journey.

Animism and spiritual cosmologies shaped the earliest human worldviews, especially from prehistoric times through early agricultural societies. These belief systems held that nature, animals, and celestial bodies were alive with spirit or consciousness. This view wasn't just religious; it was a way of life that wove the natural world into every aspect of human experience. Personally, I find this perspective powerful in its reverence for nature and its acknowledgment that humans are part of a larger, animated whole.

Culturally, animism inspired rich oral traditions, mythologies, and early art like cave paintings, which weren't just decorative but deeply symbolic, helping communities understand their place in the world. These stories and images connected generations and fostered a shared identity before the invention of writing. Communities were structured around spiritual figures such as shamans and elders, who acted as guides and healers, reinforcing social bonds through rituals tied to seasonal cycles and survival.

Without centralized governments, leadership was often spiritual or collective, rooted in a deep respect for nature and the rhythms of life. Early political and social systems were fluid and based on consensus, not coercion. Technologically, these societies developed tools and early agricultural practices that aligned with natural cycles; planting, harvesting, and hunting were seen not just as tasks, but as sacred engagements with the world.

Overall, animism instilled a sense of interconnection that influenced both survival strategies and spiritual development. This worldview laid the groundwork for later ecological awareness and spiritual traditions, reminding us of a time when humans saw the earth not as a resource to exploit, but as a community to live with.

As societies grew more complex, the limitations of decentralized, fluid social structures became more apparent, paving the way for new forms of religious and political organization. The rise of monotheism marked a profound shift not only in spiritual belief but also in how communities conceived of authority and moral order.

The rise of monotheism from the Iron Age through the Classical Period reshaped human thought by proposing that a single, all-powerful deity governs moral law and human destiny, a concept that moved beyond the fragmented loyalties of polytheism into a universal ethical framework. Judaism, Christianity, and Islam anchored this shift with standardized sacred texts like the Bible and the Quran, which served not only as spiritual guides but also as shared cultural narratives uniting diverse peoples. Monumental architecture, from soaring

European cathedrals to the intricate domes of Middle Eastern mosques, became tangible expressions of this faith, embodying communal aspiration and artistic innovation.

Sociologically, monotheism transformed identity, replacing tribe-based allegiances with a broader religious community bound by codified moral laws. This shared ethical code facilitated the coexistence of different classes and regions under one moral umbrella, a precursor, I think, to modern ideas of citizenship or global human rights. Politically, monotheistic faiths underpinned the cohesion and governance of vast empires, the Roman Empire's Christian turn and the Islamic Caliphates being prime examples, legitimizing rulers through divine mandate while also, at times, sowing conflict with pluralistic neighbours.

The development of writing systems played a crucial role in preserving and disseminating sacred texts across generations, ensuring that these religious ideas could reach wide audiences and maintain their influence over time. I find it fascinating how the ability to record and transmit these core beliefs helped cement religious authority and unify cultures in a way oral traditions alone could not.

On an evolutionary level, monotheism introduced abstract moral reasoning and a sense of historical progress, encouraging people to view their lives within a grand, divinely guided narrative. This movement toward universalism didn't just transform religious practice; it fundamentally shaped the way humans conceive of ethics, community, and their place in the world.

However, as the moral and social authority of religion solidified, a new wave of thought emerged that began to question traditional sources of authority and emphasized human autonomy and reason. This intellectual transformation would eventually culminate in the Humanist and Enlightenment movements, which redefined humanity's relationship to knowledge, power, and the divine.

Humanism and Enlightenment rationalism, spanning from the Renaissance through the 18th century, represent one of the most transformative periods in human history. Central to these movements was the belief that humans are autonomous, rational beings capable of self-determination, moral agency, and progress. This marked a profound departure from earlier eras dominated by divine providence and religious dogma, which largely dictated the course of individual lives and societies.

The emphasis on human reason and dignity ignited a cultural rebirth, most vividly seen in the arts through figures like Michelangelo, whose works celebrated the human form and experience with unprecedented realism and emotion. Philosophers such as René Descartes laid the groundwork for modern thought by advocating for methodical, skeptical inquiry into nature and existence, famously asserting "Cogito, ergo sum", "I think, therefore I am". These intellectual advances were far from isolated developments; they fuelled the Scientific Revolution, which fundamentally altered humanity's understanding of the cosmos and our place within it.

What makes this period so compelling to me is how it highlights an awakening, a collective realization of human potential and creativity that broke free from centuries of unquestioned spiritual authority.

This awakening naturally seeped into the socio-political fabric of the time, challenging the deeply entrenched feudal structures and the overwhelming authority of the Church. The belief in human reason not only questioned but actively undermined the legitimacy of unquestioned hierarchy and divine right, empowering common people to demand greater participation in public life and fostering social mobility and individual rights. This intellectual ferment fed directly into political transformation, laying the groundwork for democracy, constitutionalism, and secular governance.

The American and French Revolutions, with their emphatic declarations of liberty, equality, and fraternity, were not mere political upheavals; they were radical reimaginings of governance inspired by Enlightenment ideals. The seamless transition from challenging social order to creating new political frameworks exemplifies how the era's intellectual currents permeated all aspects of life. Personally, I find it inspiring how these ideals didn't remain abstract philosophical concepts but translated into tangible actions that reshaped entire societies, proving the power of human reason to influence not just thought but the very structures of power.

Underlying these vast cultural and political shifts were technological innovations that expanded access to knowledge and facilitated global interaction. The invention and spread of the printing press democratized information, breaking the elite's monopoly on education and fostering widespread intellectual engagement. Advances in navigation and mechanical sciences opened new horizons for exploration and commerce, knitting distant societies closer together and laying early foundations for globalization. These technological strides perfectly embodied the Enlightenment's faith in human ingenuity and empirical observation as the engines of progress.

Reflecting on this, I can't help but admire how this era represented a decisive turning point, not just in the accumulation of knowledge, but in the very way humans viewed themselves. The shift from a worldview centered on divine destiny to one focused on human potential, logic, and civic freedom marks a foundational moment for modern consciousness. While the Enlightenment had its contradictions and blind spots, its enduring legacy is a testament to the profound impact of embracing reason and autonomy as guiding principles for humanity.

Fast forward to the late 20th and early 21st centuries, where the rise of Digital Individualism and Postmodern Pluralism challenges and extends these Enlightenment legacies, emphasizing multiplicity over universality and fluidity over fixed identity. This new cultural paradigm reflects the complex, interconnected, and rapidly changing world we inhabit today.

The rise of Digital Individualism and Postmodern Pluralism from the late 20th century into the 21st century represents one of the most fascinating cultural transformations of our time. At its heart is the belief that identity is no longer something fixed or handed down from traditional authorities but instead fluid, decentralized, and deeply self-constructed. I find this shift both exhilarating and disorienting. Exhilarating because it allows unprecedented freedom to define oneself beyond rigid categories, but disorienting because it challenges the very idea of a stable, singular identity.

This mirrors the broader postmodern critique of grand narratives and universal truths, emphasizing instead that truth is contextual, often shaped and mediated by the technologies we use daily. This feels like a natural evolution, especially when we consider how the 20th century's rigid social structures have gradually given way to a world where individual stories matter more, and truth is something we negotiate rather than inherit.

Culturally, this shift has been accompanied by the rise of global pop culture and identity politics, phenomena that feel inseparable from the internet and mass media's influence. Where previous generations might have experienced identity through localized communities or nation-states, today's digital platforms create global spaces where countless decentralized narratives flourish simultaneously. This global mash-up reminds me of the civil rights movements and feminist waves that challenged dominant narratives in the last century, but now it happens at an accelerated pace and on a vast scale.

The proliferation of diverse voices online is empowering as it allows historically marginalized groups to shape their own stories rather than rely on external validation, but it also complicates the cultural landscape. The result is a kind of pluralism where unity is no longer a given, and shared cultural references are fragmented, creating both vibrant diversity and the risk of isolated echo chambers.

Sociologically, this cultural transformation coincides with the collapse of many traditional hierarchies, whether in family, work, or education. This change has shifted society's focus toward diversity, equity, mental health, and personal expression in ways that feel overdue and necessary. From my perspective, the increased attention to mental health and emotional well-being is one of the most meaningful developments. The rigid social molds of the past often forced individuals into narrow roles, suppressing complexities of identity and experience. Now, thanks partly to the influences of postmodern thought and partly to technological changes, people are freer to express their multifaceted selves.

This isn't without tension, of course, because the very structures that once offered stability are now questioned or dismantled, leaving many navigating uncertain terrain. Yet, I believe this tension is an essential part of growth. Societies evolve by breaking down old forms and exploring new possibilities.

What fascinates me most is how this sociological shift dovetails so seamlessly into technological transformation. The same forces that promote personal expression and dismantle hierarchies also fuel innovations like the internet, social media, AI, and virtual platforms, which in turn radically reshape how we communicate and experience identity. There's a continuity here: just as society moves toward more fluid, decentralized models of belonging, technology amplifies that fluidity by giving individuals unprecedented control over how they present themselves and connect with others.

These digital platforms act as arenas where identity can be curated, experimented with, and performed in multiple ways simultaneously. This isn't merely a tool but a fundamental reconfiguration of human interaction, something I find both thrilling and a bit unsettling. It's thrilling because it expands our horizons and democratizes expression; unsettling because the boundaries between real and constructed selves blur, and the constant flood of information can fragment attention and understanding.

Politically, these cultural and technological shifts translate into a redistribution of power that feels revolutionary compared to previous eras. Social movements powered by digital activism. From the Arab Spring to WikiLeaks, they illustrate how control over narratives is no longer monopolized by states or corporations. The internet has become a battleground where citizens can expose hidden truths and mobilize collective action like never before.

I see this as a deeply hopeful development. Ordinary people can challenge oppressive systems and demand accountability in ways unimaginable before the digital age. But it also brings complexity and instability. The democratization of information means we live in a world where misinformation spreads as easily as facts, and consensus is harder to achieve. This dual nature, empowering yet destabilizing, is a hallmark of our time.

Ultimately, the evolutionary impact of Digital Individualism and Postmodern Pluralism is the emergence of a hyper-connected, self-reflective consciousness that constantly questions "truth" and embraces multiplicity. In my view, this is the defining tension of the 21st century: the freedom to explore diverse perspectives and identities comes with the challenge of navigating a world without fixed anchors. This condition is both liberating and unsettling. Liberating because it opens new paths for personal and collective growth, unsettling because it demands new ways of thinking, relating, and grounding ourselves.

It requires us to cultivate critical thinking, empathy, and resilience as we adapt to a reality where change is the only constant. In this light, Digital Individualism and Postmodern Pluralism feel less like endpoints and more like ongoing experiments in what it means to be human in an interconnected, rapidly evolving world.

In embracing this four-tradition framework, from the animistic reverence of our prehistoric forebears, through the unifying moral vision of monotheism, the emancipatory promise of humanist reason, and now into the fluid terrains of digital individualism and pluralism, we gain more than a map of intellectual history; we cultivate a living appreciation for how each epoch bequeaths its insights, challenges, and urgencies to the next. By tracing these traditions as interlocking, generative phases rather than isolated chapters, we honour the deep continuity of human striving even as we acknowledge the radical transformations that propel us forward. It is my hope that, together, we continue to refine this model, not as a closed system, but as an open-ended conversation, so that we might better understand our collective past, navigate the complexities of our present, and shape a future in which the full spectrum of human consciousness can flourish.

I want to express my sincere gratitude for sharing your profound insights, Gruncle Sohail. Engaging with your perspective has deepened my own understanding and appreciation of the complex evolution of human consciousness. While our interpretations of the four traditions may diverge in certain ways, I believe it is precisely through such diverse viewpoints that we can more fully grasp the richness and dynamism of our collective journey. These traditions are not static but living frameworks that continue to inform how we understand ourselves and the world around us.

I am hopeful that this ongoing dialogue will not only illuminate the past but also inspire us to thoughtfully consider how we might navigate the challenges and opportunities of our present age. Your thoughtful analysis serves as a meaningful foundation from which we can explore these themes further. Thank you again for your openness and wisdom as I look forward to continuing this enriching conversation.

With deep respect and warm regards,
Eden

LETTER NO. 17 — EXISTENTIALISM AND HUMANISM

Dear Eden,

Thank you for sharing your profound insights about different dimensions of human evolution. I like the way you think and articulate your thoughts. Your ideas flow like a river, whispering and dancing and enlightening. I learn so many new things from your letters.

Now let me focus on two philosophies that played a significant role in shaping human consciousness of the 20th century. They are Existentialism and Humanism. They are both close to my heart so I explored their history and their impact on human psychology and psychotherapy. Let me share in this letter what I discovered.

EXISTENTIALIST PHILOSOPHY

When I think of existentialist philosophy the first name that comes to my mind is Soren Kierkegaard. Kierkegaard was a Danish philosopher who was born in 1813 and died in 1855 at the young age of 42. He is considered the first existentialist philosopher although he was not familiar with the term existentialist. He was the first scholar who stated that rather than religion or society, it is the person himself/herself who makes his/her life 'authentic'. He realized that human beings can choose not to follow hypocritical religious or prejudiced social traditions and follow their own heart to lead an authentic life.

Kierkegaard was a Christian theologian but he was quite vocal about his criticisms. When his criticisms were not taken kindly by his community he started writing with a pseudonym. Kierkegaard was opposed to state religion and considered religion as a private relationship between Man and God.

Kierkegaard wrote extensively but his diaries were not translated in French and English until the 20th century when he became popular worldwide.

Kierkegaard believed that concrete human experiences were more important than abstract religious and philosophical theories. He agreed with Buddha who has said 2500 years ago,

"One's own experience is the best teacher."

Kierkegaard, in his diaries, stated that many political activists fight political battles for freedom of expression and action not realizing that freedom of thinking was far more precious than freedom of expression and action for which we do not need external approval.

Kierkegaard was not familiar with the term Existentialism because it was coined in 1940 by French philosopher Gabriel Marcel and popularized by Jean Paul Sartre when in 1945 he presented a paper titled *Existentialism Is A Humanism.* Sartre's novel *Nausea* and Albert Camus novel *Outsider* and essay *The Myth of Sisyphus* also played a significant role in popularizing existentialism in Europe.

When existentialism became popular in philosophical circles it was also introduced by psychologists and psychotherapists in their clinical practice.

Philosophers of the existentialist school highlighted that human beings have a free will. They experience choices when they face life challenges. They can succumb to those challenges and experience ontological insecurity and existential despair or they can make wise choices and create a meaningful life for themselves and their dear ones. Let me focus on three existentialist philosophers.

The first one is Ludwig Binswanger. Binswanger (1881-1966) suggested that to understand human existence we can divide the experience into three dimensions.

1. The first dimension is human beings experiencing their inner world called Eigenwelt

2. The second dimension is human beings experiencing other human beings called Mitwelt

3. The third dimension is human beings experiencing the environment and the universe around them called Umwelt.

Binswanger had an opportunity to work with and learn from great psychologists and psychiatrists like Carl Jung, Eugene Bleuler and Sigmund Freud. He offered Freud refuge in 1938 in Switzerland.

Binswanger's contributions to human psychology, psychiatry and psychotherapy are significant as they emphasize subjective experiences of patients. Rather than judging their behaviours and interpreting their unconscious motives, Binswanger suggests that we ask our patients what meaning they give to their encounters with life. The Existentialist School of human psychology was a significant departure from the psychoanalytic school. Binswanger encouraged his patients to take control of their lives, feel empowered and make healthy choices.

The second philosopher is Karl Jaspers (1883-1969). When I was studying at Memorial University Newfoundland, one of my professors Dr. John Hoenig introduced me to Jaspers as he had translated his 1000 page German masterpiece *General*

Psychopathology into English. Jaspers helped psychiatrists and psychologists understand the concepts of phenomenology. He discussed how the symptoms of psychiatric patients can be divided into two groups:

- problems of the form
- and the problems of the content.

For example, a patient who cannot focus on his conversation and jumps from one topic to another has a formal thought disorder. On the other hand, a delusional person who believes that someone is poisoning him has a content thought disorder.

Jaspers was a great supporter of human freedom.

The third philosopher is Jean Paul Sartre (1905 – 1980). Sartre made valuable contributions to the Existentialist School. He was a writer and a philosopher. He refused to accept the Nobel Prize for Literature in 1964 stating, "a writer should not allow himself to be turned into an institution." Sartre's statement that human beings are 'condemned to be free" highlights his philosophy that we have no choice but to have a choice. Not making a choice is also making a choice. Sartre challenged many religious traditions and deterministic ideologies and asserted human freedom and choice. He focused on the philosophy that *existence precedes essence*. Human beings do not have a meaning in life other than what they give it themselves. He encouraged human beings to take responsibility for their lives and make them meaningful. His book *Being and Nothingness* and his collection of plays *No Exit* capture the essence of his philosophy. Sartre was also quite vocal about his political views. He criticized the French government about its role in Algeria. When he was arrested for his civil disobedience activities, President Charles de Gaulle set him free, stating, "You don't arrest Voltaire."

Sartre's contributions to existentialist philosophy have also influenced the disciplines of human psychology and psychotherapy. Sartre challenged Sigmund Freud and psychoanalysis and suggested that we need to focus on our present *here and now* rather than being preoccupied with the past like the psychoanalysts. Exploring our freedom in the present can set us free to have a better and happier future. Sartre's life-long love affair with a leading feminist Simone de Beauvoir was a source of inspiration for both. Sartre contributed to Simone's feminism and Simone contributed to Sartre's existentialism. Their fifty years of loving relationship ended when Sartre died in 1980. Since neither of them believed in life after death, Simone stated on Sartre's death, "Your death separated us and my death will not bring us together." Existentialist philosophers broadened the existential horizons of human psychology and added new dimensions to our understanding of the human personality.

Alongside Existentialist School of philosophy there was a parallel school of thought developing that is now known as

Humanist School of Psychology and Psychotherapy.

While many schools of human psychology focused on the sick part of the human personality, the humanist school focused on the healthy part and found ways to inspire people to express their full potential and lead a meaningful life. Of all the humanist philosophers and psychologists, let me focus on four of them.

The first humanist psychologist is Rollo May. His book *The Meaning of Anxiety* is an amazing book. It is based on May's PhD thesis. In that book he reviews many philosophical and psychological theories and suggests how people can understand and deal with their anxiety and face the dilemma of *to be or not to be*. Roll May was impressed by theologian Paul Tillich and was so inspired by his book *The Courage to Be* that he named his own book *The Courage to Create*. May believed that human beings go through four stages of development.

1. Innocence Stage. In this stage a child is not self-conscious and just follows his drives.

2. Rebellion Stage. In this stage a teenager wants to rebel to gain his freedom but has not learnt to take responsibility for his rebellion and freedom.

3. Ordinary Stage. In this stage a person learns to take responsibility but finds it too stressful, so he conforms to the social and cultural traditions to make his life easier.

4. Creative Stage. In this stage a person learns to be authentic and is ready to pay the price to be non-traditional and creative.

May also wrote a book titled *Love and Will* that captures some of his humanist ideas and ideals.

The second humanist psychologist is Carl Rogers (1902-1987). He introduced humanist principles to psychotherapy and named his therapy *Client Centered Psychotherapy*. He shared that in the traditional psychoanalytical approach, the therapist is the authority that makes interpretations. But in Client Centered Psychotherapy the patient gains more power in the therapeutic relationship. He introduced the concept of "unconditional positive regard" in therapy.

The third humanist psychologist is Abraham Maslow (1908-1970). Maslow focused on the healthy and creative part of the human personality. He wanted to know the secret of how human beings can be inspired to become fully human. He shared his theory of a *Hierarchy of Needs*. He divided human needs into five groups.

1. Physiological Needs that include food, water, sleep and sex
2. Safety Needs that include security of body and health
3. Love and Belonging Needs that include friendships, family and loving relationships.
4. Esteem Needs that include self-esteem, confidence and the respect of others.
5. Self-Actualizing Needs that include creativity and personal growth.

Maslow studied self-actualized people to discover how they satisfied their basic needs so that they could focus on their self-actualizing needs. Maslow contributed not only to the field of human psychology but also to that of human spirituality. He studied spiritual and religious experiences as a psychologist and called them *peak experiences*. He believed that human beings can have peak experiences even if they do not have any belief in God or Religion.

The fourth humanist psychologist is Victor Frankl. After spending many years in concentration camps and losing many members of his family, when he became a free man he wrote a book titled *Man's Search for Meaning*. That book became a bestseller and was translated into many languages all over the world. In that book Frankl presents his philosophy that human suffering becomes more bearable when it finds a meaning. Based on that philosophy Frankl created a therapy model that is called Logo-therapy. In *Logo-therapy* the therapist helps clients find their own unique meaning in life. Humanist psychologists and philosophers broadened the scope of human psychology. They created a holistic approach to the human condition. They inspired people to discover their unique potential and then express it so that they can lead a creative and self-actualized life.

....

Dear Eden, These schools of thought shaped my ideas and ideals as a therapist as well as a humanist. Over the years I have added new ideas to my own version of Humanism. Now I call it Seven Colours of a Humanist Rainbow. If you are interested I can share that rainbow in my next letter.

Peacefully,
Gruncle Sohail

LETTER NO. 18 — NIHILISM AND POSTMODERNISM

Dear Gruncle Sohail,

Thank you sincerely for your beautifully articulated letter. Your reflections on existentialism and humanism resonate deeply, and I am continually inspired by the depth of your philosophical and psychological insights. Your words flow with a poetic grace that both enlightens and invites profound contemplation. It is a privilege to engage in this letter exchange with you.

You have offered a rich and comprehensive overview of existentialist philosophy, from Kierkegaard's pioneering emphasis on authentic individual choice, through the multifaceted contributions of Binswanger, Jaspers, and Sartre, to the parallel humanist tradition championed by May, Rogers, Maslow, and Frankl. I appreciate your thoughtful exploration of these traditions as foundational to 20th-century psychology and psychotherapy, highlighting their shared commitment to freedom, responsibility, and meaning.

Building on your foundation, I would like to deepen our conversation by considering not only these formative philosophies but also the critical challenges and expansions introduced by nihilism and postmodernism, which together nuance and complicate the humanistic and existential narratives you described.

Existentialism's courageous assertion of radical freedom, Sartre's declaration that we are "condemned to be free," offers a powerful vision of human agency and ethical responsibility. It suggests that human beings are thrust into existence without a predetermined essence and compelled to create their own values and meaning through choice and action. This profound shift from essentialist or deterministic perspectives places the burden of meaning-making squarely on the individual, free from theological or societal imposition. Sartre's famous statement that "existence precedes essence" not only reorients philosophy but also psychology, demanding that individuals face the daunting responsibility of self-definition.

However, this vision is not without its paradoxes and challenges. While existentialism advocates for authentic self-creation, the ideal of authenticity remains an ethical horizon rather than a fixed state. The continual striving toward authenticity is as much about the process as the outcome, underscoring the fluidity and complexity of human existence. Moreover, existentialism's focus on individual freedom can unintentionally ignore or underestimate the myriad social, cultural, economic, and historical constraints that shape a person's capacity to choose. For instance, systemic issues such as racism, sexism, economic disenfranchisement, and colonial legacies limit the practical freedom individuals can exercise, casting doubt on the universality of existential freedom. This tension invites a more socially aware existentialism that recognizes freedom's embeddedness in power structures and collective histories.

Furthermore, existentialism's emphasis on a coherent, self-determining individual sometimes overlooks the fragmented and multifaceted nature of human identity. Contemporary scholars in existential psychology, as well as feminist, queer, and postcolonial theorists, have challenged the assumption of a unified self, pointing out that identity is often constructed through conflicting roles, relationships, and power dynamics. This pluralistic and intersectional understanding of identity complicates the existential notion of the self as a singular, autonomous agent and instead highlights the relational and performative aspects of subjectivity. Thus, existentialism, while liberating in its focus on freedom, may sometimes oversimplify the nuanced reality of human existence.

Kierkegaard's contributions to the discourse on the self and faith have undeniably influenced existential thought; however, from a postmodern nihilist perspective, his conceptualization of the self as a relation balancing finitude and infinity risks rectifying an essentialist notion of identity. His "leap of faith," while emphasizing individual authenticity over institutional conformity, presupposes a coherent self-capable of such existential commitment. Drawing on post-structuralist critiques, the coherence Kierkegaard attributes to the self is destabilized by the recognition that subjectivity is fragmented and socially constructed through discursive regimes and differences. Thus, the idea of an authentic self-accessible via introspection or faith is problematized as an ideological construct embedded within historical and cultural power relations.

In the realm of existential psychology, the works of Ludwig Binswanger, Karl Jaspers, and Jean-Paul Sartre are often celebrated for advancing beyond traditional psychoanalytic models by emphasizing subjective meaning, choice, and freedom. Binswanger's triadic model, Eigenwelt (self-experience), Mitwelt (experience of others), and Umwelt (experience of the environment), offers a multidimensional approach foregrounding lived experience over reductionist symptomatology. Yet, from a postmodern perspective, this framework may inadvertently reinforce a metanarrative of a stable, coherent self-interacting meaningfully with its environment, a notion challenged by the recognition of identity's multiplicity and fragmentation.

Similarly, Jaspers' phenomenological differentiation between form and content in psychopathology and his focus on existential choice presuppose a degree of agency and self-awareness that postmodern critiques problematize. The therapeutic goal of facilitating "authentic existence" presumes the possibility of accessing a foundational self beyond social and linguistic mediation, an assumption challenged by Judith Butler's theory of performativity, which posits identity as constituted through repeated social enactments rather than an inherent essence.

Sartre's philosophical insistence on radical freedom and responsibility confronts deterministic psychoanalytic paradigms and highlights the ethical dimensions of choice. However, postmodern nihilism calls into question the ontological status of such freedom and the coherence of the "self" that exercises it. Moreover, Sartre's ethical imperative to choose "for humanity" relies on a concept of a unified human essence or collective subjectivity that postmodern thought deconstructs as a discursive formation rather than an ontological given. This critique aligns with the skepticism toward humanist universalism that characterizes much postmodern philosophy.

While existentialist philosophers and psychologists have significantly shaped modern understandings of selfhood, freedom, and meaning, a postmodern nihilist critique emphasizes the contingency, fragmentation, and discursive construction of these concepts. This perspective problematizes the foundational assumptions of existentialism and humanism, particularly the coherence of the self, the primacy of freedom, and the possibility of authentic existence. It suggests instead that these are historically situated and culturally contingent constructs rather than universal or foundational truths.

Humanistic psychology emerged as a hopeful corrective to the psychoanalytic and behaviorist focus on pathology. Rollo May's stages of development, from innocence through rebellion, conformity, to creativity, capture the complexity of growing into authentic adulthood. May's notion that anxiety can be a creative force, a signal of existential engagement rather than mere pathology, invites a more dynamic understanding of mental health and human potential. His work situates anxiety not as something to be eliminated but as a vital impetus for growth and meaning.

Carl Rogers' Client-Centered Therapy revolutionized psychotherapy by emphasizing unconditional positive regard and the client's inherent capacity for growth. Rogers' model democratized the therapeutic relationship and affirmed the self's potential for healing, aligning closely with humanism's optimistic view of human nature as fundamentally constructive and striving toward fulfillment. His focus on empathy, congruence, and genuineness in the therapeutic encounter has had a profound influence on modern counseling and broader understandings of human relationships.

Abraham Maslow's hierarchy of needs offers a structured vision of human motivation, culminating in self-actualization. His studies of "peak experiences" foreground spirituality and transcendence, showing how psychology can embrace rather than exclude the profound and ineffable aspects of human experience. Maslow's work bridged psychology and spirituality, offering a framework for understanding human flourishing that transcends mere survival or social conformity. His notion of self-actualization as a lifelong process rather than a fixed achievement encourages a hopeful vision of continuous growth and the pursuit of meaning.

Victor Frankl's logotherapy powerfully asserts that even in the direst suffering, humans can find meaning. His emphasis on meaning as the primary motivational force broadens the therapeutic task beyond symptom relief to existential engagement. Frankl's lived experience in Nazi concentration camps and subsequent clinical work provide compelling evidence for the human capacity to endure and transcend hardship through purpose. His famous idea that "he who has a way to live can bear almost any how" encapsulates the central role of meaning in resilience.

Yet, humanism's optimism faces challenges in light of cultural relativism and systemic critique. The model of a coherent, self-actualizing individual reflects a largely Western, liberal ideal that may not universally apply. For example, collectivist cultures often prioritize relational harmony and communal well-being over individual autonomy, complicating the universal applicability of humanist therapy models. Additionally, humanism's focus on individual growth sometimes neglects the social, political, and economic barriers that hinder self-expression and well-being for many marginalized populations. Addressing these critiques requires an expanded humanism that is culturally sensitive and socially aware, integrating collective and structural dimensions of human experience.

While existentialism and humanism seek to affirm freedom and meaning, nihilism confronts their absence. Nihilism, often misunderstood as mere despair, can also be understood as a radical honesty about the void, acknowledging that no inherent meaning, value, or purpose exists in the universe. Friedrich Nietzsche's diagnosis of "the death of God" highlights the cultural crisis of losing transcendent foundations for meaning. Nietzsche did not simply lament this loss but called for a revaluation of values and the creation of new life-affirming ideals, embodied in the figure of the Übermensch, a symbol of creative self-overcoming and the forging of new meaning in a godless world.

Nihilism's importance lies in its critique of all absolutes and its refusal to settle for false consolations. For marginalized and oppressed peoples, nihilism can serve as a mode of resistance against dominant ideologies and imposed meanings that exclude or dehumanize them. In this light, nihilism is not just despair but a site of potential freedom and creativity, though one that requires courage to inhabit and transform. Recognizing nihilism's creative potential opens pathways for new existential and ethical possibilities beyond despair.

In contemporary psychology, nihilism challenges clinicians and patients to grapple honestly with existential emptiness and to explore meaning-making as a creative, ongoing process rather than a given fact. Therapeutic approaches that acknowledge nihilism invite a dialectical process between meaning and meaninglessness, hope and despair, presence and absence. This nuanced engagement with nihilism can deepen psychological resilience and foster richer existential awareness.

Postmodernism further complicates the existential and humanist project by questioning the very concepts of "self," "truth," and "freedom" as stable or universal. Philosophers such as Michel Foucault, Jacques Derrida, and Jean-François Lyotard have shown how knowledge and identity are constructed through language, power relations, and cultural narratives. The postmodern critique highlights the contingency and multiplicity of truths and identities, resisting totalizing or essentialist accounts. This perspective urges humility and openness in philosophical and therapeutic inquiry, recognizing the partiality and situatedness of all knowledge.

In psychotherapy, postmodern approaches emphasize narrative, deconstruction, and the co-construction of meaning between therapist and client. This paradigm shift encourages a flexible, context-sensitive understanding of identity and experience. It also underscores the ethical responsibility of therapists to be aware of the power dynamics inherent in therapeutic relationships. By fostering dialogue rather than prescription, postmodern therapy honours the client's unique story and relational context.

The postmodern insight into the fragmented self resonates with contemporary understandings from neuroscience and social psychology, which depict identity as fluid, socially embedded, and constantly reconstructed. This challenges existentialism's and humanism's assumptions of a unitary, autonomous self, urging a more relational and pluralistic perspective. Embracing this complexity allows psychology and philosophy to more fully engage with the lived realities of identity in a globalized and diverse world.

Taken together, existentialism, humanism, nihilism, and postmodernism offer complementary and sometimes conflicting perspectives on the human condition. Existentialism invites us to confront freedom and responsibility; humanism inspires hope in human potential; nihilism demands honesty about meaning's absence; postmodernism deconstructs the very frameworks we use to understand ourselves. A nuanced human psychology must integrate these voices, recognizing that human beings live at the intersection of freedom and constraint, meaning and absurdity, unity and fragmentation. Therapeutically, this means honoring each individual's unique narrative, contextualizing suffering and growth within social realities, and embracing ambiguity without despair.

Your mention of the "Seven Colours of Humanist Rainbow" over dinner caught my attention as a beautiful way to express the rich diversity and pluralism of human experience. Although I am not yet familiar with the full details of your concept, I am genuinely curious about how you envision these colours representing different facets or dimensions of humanism. I look forward to hearing your insights on how this metaphor can deepen our understanding of human potential and complexity, perhaps offering a fresh perspective on the interplay between individuality and commonality within the human condition.

With warmest regards,

Eden

LETTER NO. 19 — A HUMANIST RAINBOW

Dear Eden,

Thank you for juxtra-posing philosophies of nihilism and postmodernism with existentialism and humanism and highlighting the similarities and differences of these schools of thoughts. In some ways they are supporting and cooperating and in other ways they are conflicting and contradicting each other. Together they represent the dark and bright sides of human thinking and human condition. They are human attempts to make life meaningful.

Albert Camus, in his essay *Myth of Sisyphus* states that the biggest philosophical human problem in the issue of suicide. Just because life might seem meaningless does not mean that we kill ourselves. Life might be meaningless but it is still not worthless. We need to learn to enjoy and cherish life.

Dear Eden,

From an abstract academic discussion let me come back to personal and philosophical discussion.

I grew up in conservative, religious and traditional culture of Pakistan and then moved to a secular, liberal and democratic culture of Canada and became a humanist psychotherapist.

After saying goodbye to God and religion, I embraced Humanism but for me that tradition was more than a set of ideas, it had many dimensions. Over the years and decades I have discovered 7 colours of my humanistic rainbow

FIRST COLOUR...HUMANIST PHILOSOPHY

Over the years I realized that to become a humanist I had to leave blind faith behind and study science and philosophy so that I could develop logical and rational thinking and use critical thinking to question all the myths and supernatural teachings of my family, community and culture. In this journey writings of Charles Darwin, Karl Marx, Sigmund Freud, Bertrand Russell, Jean Paul Sartre and many other philosophers paved my way to my acceptance of atheism and humanism. I am glad that humanist philosophy helped me in making rational and responsible choices for myself and communicating with others who have a scientific attitude towards life.

SECOND COLOUR...HUMANIST PERSONALITY

When I realized that people's behaviours may not be a true reflection of their belief system and their personality may not be in harmony with their philosophy, I started paying more attention to people's behaviours and personalities. Now I have come to the awareness that a humanist personality reflected in a caring, kind and compassionate attitude might be seen in different people with different ideologies and philosophies. As compared to humanistic personality some people have a fundamentalist personality that is very critical, judgmental and aggressive. People with such personality try to convert others and get angry and have bitter debates with their opponents. It is quite amazing for me to see how some religious people have a humanist personality while there are some atheists who have a fundamentalist personality. Over the years I have tried to develop a humanist personality alongside acquiring a humanist philosophy.

THIRD COLOUR...HUMANIST LIFESTYLE

After developing a humanist philosophy and striving to have a humanist personality, I realized that both of them had to be actualized in a humanist lifestyle. When I put my philosophy and personality in practice I realized that other humanists welcomed it but it created a tension with the traditional friends and religious families I knew. I had to learn to be tolerant and accepting of their truth. It was a struggle to accept the reality that my truth is *a truth* and not *the truth*. It was a test for me to accept that other human beings have the right to their ideology and philosophy as long as they do not impose it on me or stop me from practicing my truth. In this transition I lost some of my relatives and friends who could not accept my humanism and associated atheism with an immoral and unethical life. Now I have a circle of friends from different cultures and backgrounds who are respectful of each other's philosophy and are willing to have a meaningful dialogue. They belong to my Family of the Heart.

Now I realize that there are as many truths as human beings and as many realities as pairs of eyes in this world.

FOURTH COLOUR...HUMANIST PSYCHOTHERAPY

As I accepted my own truth and felt confident to acknowledge it publicly in my social life, I also introduced humanist philosophy to my clinical practice. Reading the writings of Eric Fromm, Carl Rogers, Victor Frankl and Abraham Maslow helped me at a conceptual and philosophical level to accept my patient's experiences and truths and then help them decrease their suffering and improve their quality of life. Such a journey helped me create my unique clinical practice of my Creative Psychotherapy Clinic and with the help of my colleagues Anne Henderson and Bette Davis write a series of books about my Green Zone Philosophy. Such a philosophy and practice has helped me in helping my patients to develop a kind, caring and compassionate personality. I helped them in trusting their intelligence and conscience more than the religious traditions of their families and communities that contributed to their concept of sin and feelings of guilt. Therapy also helped them either resolve their social conflicts with their religious relatives or dissolve their relationships with relatives and friends who have a fundamentalist personality. As therapy evolved they were able to create a healthy, happy and peaceful lifestyle. I feel very excited that now we have created a website www.greenzoneliving.ca

And videos and books so that more and more people can benefit from a Green Zone Philosophy and develop a humanist personality and lifestyle.

FIFTH COLOUR... HUMANIST EDUCATION

After I realized that my religious upbringing had negatively affected my personality and had introduced me to the concept of sin producing feelings of guilt about sex and many other things and it took me years even decades to unlearn those values, I tried to share with others that it might be wise to teach religious traditions of the world at homes and in schools as a part of history rather than a part of their faith. Parents and teachers have the responsibility to pass on collective knowledge and wisdom to the next generation so that children can make rational and responsible choices for their own lives as adults. I had to share with parents and teachers that humanist values can be taught even without wrapping them in religious and faith based practices. It is encouraging to see that more and more parents and teachers are realizing that education based on secular values married to science, philosophy and psychology encourages children in developing a rational, critical and creative mind. They are becoming aware that education is different from indoctrination.

SIXTH COLOUR ...HUMANIST COMMUNITIES

Since I am a poet and a writer alongside a psychotherapist, I became involved in the social and political dialogues of different groups in Pakistan and Canada. It has been my experience that as more and more people become aware of the effects of religion on people and how different religious and political leaders exploit and abuse the concepts of God and Religion to create holy wars between different sects and different religions, it is important for freethinkers to try their best to raise social consciousness. Being a writer I have written many essays and books on these subjects and translated writings of atheist and humanist philosophers in Urdu so that we can promote humanism through education in Urdu speaking men and women. I receive many emails from South Asia and the

Middle East from men and women who read my essays on the website www.humsub.com.pk

And share their struggles. I feel that free thinkers need moral support as they are in the minority and need a group where they can share their struggles and get into meaningful dialogues while they are in search of their truth. Creating a secular community is an essential part of humanism so that there is not only freedom *of* religion but also freedom *from* religion. There are many communities all over the world that have very punitive traditions and persecutory laws against non-believers. In some communities atheists are afraid to be killed by religious zealots. Such an oppressive environment forces people to become hypocrites and not share their truth openly and honestly and lead a double life.

SEVENTH COLOUR...HUMANIST CULTURE

It is my dream that we reach such a stage in human evolution where we can see a humanist culture all over the world. I am of the opinion that the unresolved conflicts of class, gender, race, sexual orientation, language, nationality and religion continue to be the cause of human suffering and we need to work together to create a just and a humanist culture. Such a culture will help all of us to become fully human individually and collectively.

I am well aware that these are the colours of my humanist dream but I also know that we all have to dream before the dream comes true. We need a critical mass of humanists who are dedicated and committed and willing to work together to create humanist traditions in their families, schools and communities. It is encouraging to read that in 1900 only 1% people publicly acknowledged that they did not believe in God and organized religions and in 2000 the number had increased to 20% internationally. Scandinavian countries have more than 50% people who have embraced humanist philosophy.

As the numbers grow, I become more hopeful that my humanist dream will come true.

Dear Eden,

Let me share a short poem that captures the essence of my humanist philosophy. It is titled

PEACE

There in inner peace and there is outer peace

There is emotional peace and there is social peace

There is religious peace and there is political peace

There is local peace and there is global peace

These are all colours of peace

And we need all these colours to create a rainbow of peace.

Dear Eden,

I have shared with you the summary of my philosophy of life. Now I would like you to share the essence of your philosophy of life so that we can move towards concluding this discussion and completing our joint book.

Affectionately,
Gruncle Sohail

LETTER NO. 20 — MY PHILOSOPHY OF LIFE

Dear Gruncle Sohail,

Thank you sincerely for sharing the luminous trajectory of your personal journey and unveiling the seven vibrant colours of your humanist rainbow. This metaphor transcends mere description and invites us into a lived philosophy of compassion, critical inquiry, and radical empathy. Your ability to interweave rigorous intellectual reflection with kindness and a profound respect for the plurality of human experience exemplifies humanism not only as an abstract worldview but as a transformative praxis. In an era often marked by polarization, dogmatism, and reductive binaries, your emphasis on tolerance and respect for divergent truths radiates a hopeful vision. In this vision, humanism emerges as a dynamic force for personal liberation and collective flourishing.

Your ongoing work to help others disentangle themselves from debilitating webs of guilt, shame, and self-reproach, encouraging instead a life informed by reason, kindness, and care, is deeply inspiring. It models the ideal of humanism as a philosophy both intellectually honest and profoundly humane. Your poem "PEACE," with its resonant invocation of multiple layers of peace, inner, interpersonal, and societal, beautifully captures the complexity of the peace we must cultivate to build

a world that honours our shared humanity. It reminds me that peace is not a simplistic endpoint but a continual, collective project requiring humility, openness, and courage.

With this spirit of embracing complexity, ambiguity, and the coexistence of multiple, often conflicting truths, I would like to share with you how my own philosophical journey has unfolded over the years and continues to evolve. It has evolved in conversation with both the pain and promise of my lived experience and with the broader intellectual currents shaping contemporary thought.

My philosophical inquiry began in childhood, deeply shaped by a scientific upbringing that instilled in me an early fascination with fundamental questions of existence: why we are here and what, if anything, gives life meaning. In the sterile empirical world of science, where laws govern phenomena but offer no easy solace for the human heart, I found a paradoxical space of both certainty and profound uncertainty. It was within this tension that my search for meaning commenced.

Childhood was not only a time of intellectual curiosity but also of existential turmoil. I was confronted by waves of depression and anxiety that cast a shadow over my sense of self and future. I sought philosophical frameworks that might illuminate or at least alleviate this pervasive sense of emptiness.

Existentialism, particularly the versions championed by Jean-Paul Sartre and Albert Camus, initially offered a compelling response. Their emphasis on radical freedom and on the individual's responsibility to forge meaning in an indifferent universe resonated powerfully.

As a WOC teenager who challenges traditional belief systems grappling with cultural alienation and systemic marginalization, the existentialist proposition that meaning is not handed down from any transcendent source but must be actively self-fashioned was empowering. It suggested an emancipatory autonomy in the face of inherited narratives that often excluded or pathologized identities like mine. Sartre's notion that existence precedes essence, that we are condemned to freedom yet thereby empowered to define ourselves, spoke to a deep yearning for agency amidst cultural dislocation and familial expectations.

Yet, as I engaged more deeply with canonical existentialism, I encountered its limitations. The classical existentialist subject, a free, autonomous individual, is often implicitly imagined as white, male, and Western. It abstracts freedom from the material, social, and historical conditions that shape subjectivity. The existentialist ideal begins from a metaphysical "nothingness" or radical lack, presuming a blank slate from which to create oneself anew.

My lived reality, however, was saturated with external impositions and pre-existing meanings: cultural traditions, familial obligations, normative assumptions about gender and sexuality, and the weight of systemic structures of oppression and marginalization. I inhabited what might be described as an "overdetermined" subjectivity, a self not free to simply transcend but one embedded in dense networks of social expectation, power relations, and inherited trauma. My freedom was circumscribed, not absolute.

This dissonance revealed to me existentialism's blind spots. Its heroic narrative of self-creation, while rhetorically potent, risked becoming a form of subtle victim-blaming. By emphasizing authenticity and personal responsibility, existentialism can inadvertently place the burden of overcoming systemic injustice and mental anguish squarely on the individual's shoulders. The call to create meaning from suffering becomes not only a moral imperative but also an additional source of guilt for those who struggle. If one cannot authentically fashion their selfhood, are they then a failure? The psychological weight of such a question is immense.

Moreover, existentialism's faith in the possibility of meaning construction felt increasingly tenuous when confronted with the harsh realities of systemic violence, intergenerational trauma, and persistent social injustice. The universe's silence in the face of profound suffering seemed not merely absurd but callously indifferent. In this silence, existentialist optimism appeared as a form of denial, a philosophical coping mechanism that glossed over the entrenched structural and historical conditions constraining freedom and flourishing.

This growing disillusionment precipitated a gradual turn toward more radical philosophical pessimism and nihilism, traditions often marginalized or misunderstood as mere despair or intellectual defeatism. Thinkers such as Arthur Schopenhauer, Friedrich Nietzsche, especially in his darker moods, and Emil Cioran provided frameworks that embraced the futility inherent in the human condition without relying on the consolatory narratives of existentialism.

Schopenhauer's philosophy, often regarded as the prototypical philosophical pessimism, depicted life as an endless striving driven by the insatiable "will to live," which inevitably leads to suffering. His emphasis on desire as the root of suffering suggested that attempts to find lasting meaning or satisfaction through worldly pursuits were ultimately futile. This sobering analysis resonated deeply with my own experiences of anxiety and longing, illustrating how the pursuit of meaning can itself be a source of anguish.

Nietzsche's complex thought oscillated between profound affirmation and profound despair. While he is often celebrated as a philosopher of life-affirmation and the "will to power," his writings also explore the abyss beneath such affirmation. His concept of the eternal recurrence, a test of one's capacity to embrace life in its totality, poses a formidable challenge. In his more melancholic moments, Nietzsche acknowledged the devastating implications of the "death of God" for traditional values and meaning, prefiguring the nihilism that many philosophers have grappled with since.

Emil Cioran's unflinching recognition of meaning-making as a desperate attempt to mask the void resonated deeply. His aphoristic style, steeped in skepticism and melancholy, articulated the paradox of human consciousness, the simultaneous curse and gift of awareness forever haunted by the absence of inherent meaning. Similarly, Thomas Ligotti's suggestion, drawing on horror philosophy, that consciousness itself might be a tragic accident endowed nihilism with an existential honesty absent from more hopeful philosophies. His work challenges the assumption that consciousness is necessarily an evolutionary triumph, instead proposing it as a source of profound existential suffering.

This philosophical evolution did not represent a nihilistic capitulation but rather a rejection of the moral imperative to justify existence through meaning. Nihilism, thus constructed, functions not as despair but as a space of relief, an acknowledgment of the limits of human reason and the often overwhelming absurdity of life. It permits an honest confrontation with suffering and absurdity without demanding that pain be redeemed or identities be made coherent within some grand narrative of resilience.

Importantly, this perspective challenges dominant cultural and philosophical expectations that trauma must culminate in transformation, catharsis, or transcendence. Instead, it allows for the legitimacy of survival, endurance, and existence on their own terms, without external justification or metaphysical consolation.

This shift toward a grounded nihilism has not entailed disengagement from political or ethical commitments. On the contrary, it has fostered a praxis rooted in relational care, situated resistance, and collective solidarity, unmoored from metaphysical mandates or teleological hopes.

By acknowledging the structural violence inherent in imposed meanings and the limits of radical self-authorship under systemic constraints, this orientation embraces humility and interdependence. It insists that political struggle and ethical care must be undertaken not in service of some ultimate meaning or grand narrative but as acts of solidarity and survival in a fractured world.

Such a praxis draws inspiration from intersectional feminist, decolonial, and critical race theories, which highlight how identity categories, power relations, and socio-historical contexts shape subjectivity and constrain agency. These frameworks compel a reconsideration of classical assumptions about freedom, authenticity, and individualism, emphasizing instead relationality, situatedness, and the complex interplay of oppressions.

Incorporating these critiques enriches my understanding of humanism and compels a philosophy that is both humble and vigilant. It acknowledges that the quest for meaning and authenticity cannot ignore historical trauma, systemic inequality, and cultural displacement. Instead of idealizing freedom as pure self-creation, this framework insists on solidarity as a condition of possibility for any genuine ethical or political action.

In sum, my philosophical journey from existentialism to nihilism is neither a retreat into despair nor an abandonment of intellectual rigor. It is a movement toward a philosophy that is materially and socially grounded, one that refuses the cultural and philosophical demand to justify existence through meaning or triumph. This philosophy affirms instead the legitimacy of care, resistance, and survival on their own terms.

It embraces complexity, ambiguity, and multiplicity, themes you so eloquently capture in your humanist rainbow. It insists that peace, justice, and flourishing are not abstract ideals to be achieved once and for all but ongoing, collective practices shaped by historical and social realities.

Your vision offers a powerful counterpoint and complement to my own evolving thought. Together, your commitment to kindness, critical thinking, and respect for diverse truths, and my grappling with the limits of meaning and the imperative of care, form a dialogical space rich with possibility. In that spirit, I look forward to continuing this conversation with you.

With deep gratitude and warm regards,
Eden

LETTER NO. 21 — DEEP LOVE

Dear Eden,

Thank you for sharing your philosophy with me. After reading your last letter, I have no doubt that you are a philosopher [lover of wisdom].

It was an honour to have such an intellectually stimulating and philosophically inspiring written dialogue with you. Before I go, I want to share two creations with you that I wrote a few years ago. One deals with letter writing and my special connection with my father titled *Deep Love*, the other deals with a special connection that we all share with each other as human beings.

Peacefully,
Gruncle Sohail

DEEP LOVE

One of my childhood memories is watching my dad Basit writing 10 to 15 pages long letters to my uncle Arif. By that time my dad had become a mystic, a deeply religious person and people used to call him *Sufi Sahib*, while my uncle was still an atheist and a socialist writer. My uncle never responded to my dad's letters. I remember one day teasing my dad by saying, "Dad, Uncle Arif never responds because he never reads them." He smiled and said, "Son, they are love letters, not business letters."

After ten years of receiving my dad's long letters, when my uncle published his new collection of poems he dedicated it to my dad. That dedication reflected to me that not only he read those letters; he read them very carefully and was inspired by them. Later on my uncle also became a mystic poet.

Over the years I have been reflecting about my dad's long letters. I think most brothers, who did not get any response, would have stopped writing those letters. But my dad did not and I wondered:

What kept him writing?

What was his motivation?

Why did he not get discouraged?

Why did he not stop?

My own answer to my own prolonged reflections and introspections is *Deep Love.*

My dad loved my uncle at a deep level, deeper than most brothers I know love their brothers. Those were emotional as well as philosophical letters. My dad shared his knowledge, experience and wisdom. He shared his spiritual insights. That is why once my uncle said to me, 'Your dad is younger in age but older in wisdom. He is a man of integrity."

As a student of human psychology I ask myself, "How did my dad develop that capacity of deep love?" I think his emotional crisis has something to do with it, a crisis that family members thought was a nervous breakdown but he believed it was a spiritual breakthrough. After that crisis when he recovered and became a mystic his capacity to love became more intense, more profound. He developed a capacity for deep love. I was fortunate to receive that deep love from him too.

While I am reflecting and freely associating my dad's breakdown and breakthrough and deep love, I am also remembering a time when our neighbours were digging a well in the courtyard. As a child I was fascinated to watch that. As there was no running water in our neighbourhood and people got water from a nearby river, it was important for the neighbours to dig a well. After digging a few feet we saw the water. I was thrilled. I thought the project was complete. But my dad told me that they had to dig more because that water was good to wash clothes but not good enough to drink as it was full of impurities. After digging another twenty feet there was another layer of water at a deep level. That water was clean and good enough to drink.

I sometimes wonder whether people's hearts also have two kinds of love: superficial love and deep love. Most people can only experience and share superficial love. There are only a few, like my dad, who are able to experience and share deep love and sometimes to reach that deeper love they have to experience a breakdown and a breakthrough. Some reach that deep love on their own by life experiences, some need a teacher and some need a therapist. I have seen many men and women in my clinical practice who were able to get in touch with deep love in their hearts after they recovered from their personal, marital, family, social and existential crisis. I feel honoured that those people shared with me their honest feelings and struggles and I was able to become a co-traveler in their therapeutic journeys. Such change is only possible when therapy is dynamic and addresses some in-depth issues of personality transformation and growth. Over the years I have become a dynamic therapist and love working with those motivated people who have serious emotional and personality problems and are willing to take the next step in life in their personal growth and social maturity and get in touch with their deeper selves and experience and share deep love. I have learnt so much from them.

Reflecting back on my life I realize that receiving deep love from my dad and sharing it with my patients has helped me become a better person and serve my community and humanity at large as a humanist psychotherapist.

A VERY SPECIAL CONNECTION

You and I

    Have a connection

        A special connection

            A very special connection

It is not a sexual, romantic or physical connection

    It is rather an emotional, spiritual and creative connection

Such a connection

    Cannot be defined

        It transcends all definitions

            It brings out the best in both of us

As two human beings

    We are not only connected to each other

        We are also connected to other human beings

With passage of time

    More and more people are becoming aware

        Each human being is connected to the whole humanity

The way

    Each tree is connected to the jungle

    Each flower is connected to the garden

    Each star is connected to the galaxy

And

    Each drop is connected to the ocean

It is an intimate connection

    A loving connection

      A magical connection

        A mystical connection

          A sacred connection

            A human connection

One day we will realize

    We are all

      Part of the same family

        The human family.

CLOSING STATEMENT

Dear Reader,

Thank you for joining me on this journey. Reaching the final page of this book feels both surreal and deeply meaningful. At sixteen years old, I never imagined I would co-author a book, let alone with someone as accomplished and respected as Dr. Khalid Sohail. Yet, through encouragement, trust, and a shared vision, we made this unlikely collaboration a reality.

I want to express my heartfelt gratitude to Dr. Sohail. His wisdom, patience, and belief in me made all the difference. He is not only a brilliant thinker and writer but also a kind and generous human being. Despite being a globally respected figure with decades of experience in psychology, philosophy, and literature, and being 72 years old, he treated me, a teenager just beginning to find my voice, as an equal partner. That kind of humility and openness is rare, and it left a profound impression on me.

He gave me the space to express my thoughts, welcomed my ideas without judgment, and encouraged me to explore my deepest questions with courage and curiosity. Working with him taught me more than I could ever have learned in a classroom. I saw firsthand that wisdom is not just about knowledge but also about the ability to listen, to collaborate, and to uplift others. For that, I am endlessly grateful.

This book was not written under ideal circumstances. Right before working on it, my father suffered multiple strokes, my mother struggled with depression and anxiety, and I experienced a psychotic breakdown that led to a suicide attempt. There were moments when it felt impossible to keep going, when the weight of it all seemed too much to bear. But I did continue, and writing became a source of healing and strength.

I could not have done this without the support of my parents. My mother stood by me emotionally and physically, even while facing her own mental health challenges. Her quiet strength and unwavering presence held me together during my most fragile moments. My father, through his recovery, continued to guide me with the perspective and clarity that come from a lifetime of deep thinking. As a socialist and Trotskyist, he helped shape my worldview, not by imposing his beliefs, but by encouraging me to explore and think critically. Both of my parents gave me the freedom to grow into myself. They never forced traditional beliefs onto me and never made me feel like I had to follow a set path. Instead, they nurtured my curiosity and supported me as I carved out my own.

Their acceptance and belief in me are the reasons I was able to accomplish something like this at such a young age. I want to take this moment to thank them not only for their support, but for raising me with the values and strength that made this project possible.

There are a few things in my life that I never imagined I would be able to achieve. One was completing the United Nations Young Leaders Training Program with a 100% score, despite being the only high school student among a group of graduate students. Another was saving my father's life twice by recognizing the signs of his strokes and getting him to the hospital in time. And finally, co-authoring this book during one of the most difficult periods of my life.

Each of these experiences has taught me something essential about perseverance. True resilience is not about being unaffected by hardship, but about continuing forward in the face of it. I have learned that pain can be a powerful teacher, that personal growth often comes from our most difficult moments, and that there is strength in vulnerability.

If there is one message I hope you take away from this book, it is that your challenges do not define your limits. No matter how overwhelming life may feel, there is always a way forward. I hope this book inspires you to reflect, to remain curious, and to continue your own journey of growth and self-discovery. May it encourage you to seek wisdom, to ask difficult questions, and to believe in your ability to overcome adversity and realize your full potential.

Thank you again for being a part of this journey. :)

With gratitude,

Eden

REVIEWS

ZUBAIR KHAWAJA'S REVIEW

From Wonder to Wisdom is not just a book. It is a living conversation. A conversation between generations, cultures, ideologies, and disciplines. It brings together psychology, philosophy, science, anthropology, and personal reflections in a way that feels less like reading and more like being invited into a deeply meaningful exchange. The book itself, like the people who wrote it and the people reading it, is going through its own evolution.

No conversation about this book would be complete without recognizing the towering presence of Dr. Khalid Sohail. He is a psychiatrist, author, humanist, and one of the most prolific and thoughtful minds in Canada. With over 50 years of experience in psychiatry, literature, and global human rights discourse, Dr. Sohail has touched the lives of thousands, not just through his clinical work, but through the countless essays, poems, and books he has written to promote self-awareness, emotional healing, and intellectual freedom. His work bridges East and West, reason and emotion, science and spirit.

To me, he is more than a psychiatrist or a writer; he is a generational thinker whose voice has quietly shaped my life. I first encountered his work as a teenager in Pakistan, when the only books I had known were school textbooks, children's tales, and religious scriptures. The first book I ever truly chose to read was a translated volume about Jean-Paul Sartre's essays, which introduced me to philosophy, political struggle, and existential thought. Tucked within its pages was an essay by Dr. Khalid Sohail. I had no idea then that the voice that stirred my young mind would one day belong to the man sitting with me in our living room, discussing life and meaning, and that he would eventually co-author a book with my own daughter. That is not just a full circle; it is an orbit. Over the years, my admiration for him has only deepened. He has been a guide to many, a gentle provocateur of minds, and a warm, grounded friend.

There is a sense of pride, mixed with a touch of embarrassment, in seeing Eden publish her first book at 16, when I was only just discovering how to read a book for pleasure and meaning at that age. But that is how progress is supposed to work. We do not just raise our children. We try to give them a head start in every way we can. Eden's growth is the result of careful thought and intention. She was not an accident, nor a gift from some higher power, but the product of deliberate parenting rooted in love, structure, and awareness of the world.

Her mother, a creative spirit with a heart grounded in Sufi tradition and literature, shaped Eden's quiet strength, patience, and insight. I contributed what I could, a commitment to political awareness, social justice, and scientific reasoning. You could say Eden is the product of Sufism and Socialism. And despite the humour in that phrase, it is also true in a very real way.

We only decided to have a child once we felt we had created the right environment for her to grow, physically, intellectually, and emotionally. From the beginning, Eden was different. As a toddler, she spent more time observing than playing. Her quietness was so noticeable that her mother took her to a doctor, concerned that something might be wrong. But Eden was not disengaged. She was watching and analyzing. Her first word was not "mama" or "papa." It was "scrumptious." I did not even know if it was a real word. I had to Google it. I was surprised at how a child so young had learned that word and even used it within the right context. That one word told us all we needed to know about how her mind worked.

Even as a child, her posture was one of silent resistance, often making a tiny left-handed solidarity fist while staring intensely at the world around her. I always had a feeling that her future would involve activism, law, research, or some combination of all three. That kind of curiosity cannot be taught. It has to be nurtured.

Coming from a conservative and religious society, I knew that one of my responsibilities as a father was to shield my daughter from the kind of religious trauma I had experienced. Not by forcing atheism or ideology onto her, but by creating space for her to think for herself. Her mother gave her the freedom to explore spirituality. I made sure she had the tools to question it all scientifically. When she learned religious concepts at school, I would sit down with her and explain the origins and social functions behind them. Bedtime stories were rarely about princesses or fairy tales. Instead, we discussed politics, philosophy, and the nature of the universe.

When I had a stroke, many people told me I should be grateful to God that I survived. But the truth is, it was not divine intervention. It was Eden's intelligence, calmness, and quick decision-making that saved my life. She recognized the signs and took action. Her strength did not come from prayer. It came from knowledge.

We have known Dr. Khalid Sohail for over ten years now. We have read and discussed many of his articles and books. Eden was always quietly present in those discussions, rarely participating. But when Dr. Sohail's book *Salik* (the Urdu translation of *The Seeker*) came out, we read it together as a bedtime book. Eden responded to it with a heartfelt review, which was later featured in the introduction of this book. That moment broke the silence between her and Dr. Sohail and eventually led to this beautiful collaboration.

Books, like people, are shaped by history. Paper-bound books emerged in medieval times, but widespread reading among the general population did not begin until the 1930s, when education became a political and economic priority after the Great Depression. Now, five generations later, we find ourselves at a crossroads. Books are quietly vanishing again, not from lack of printing presses, but from lack of attention. In their place, we have instant content, viral videos, and digital distractions.

If we think of human evolution as a single calendar year, books have existed for just 8.5 hours. Literacy as a mass phenomenon has existed for even less. That means if you are reading this book, you are engaging in one of the rarest and most important acts in our species' history. You are here, living in the best 8.5 hours of human existence.

From Wonder to Wisdom is not just a book. It is a time capsule, a dialogue, a legacy. It holds within it the wisdom of an experienced philosopher and the unfiltered curiosity of a young thinker. It is filled with reflections that span continents and generations. It bridges the old and the new, the spiritual and the scientific, the personal and the political.

It is rare to read a book that not only changes you, but also contains you. Your past, your beliefs, your journey, your family. For me, this book is all of that and more.

So if you are holding this book in your hands, I congratulate you. You are a part of a story that started thousands of years ago, and one that may not last forever. But for now, for these 8.5 hours, we are here, reading, evolving, and thinking.

Welcome to the best part of human history.

~Zubair Khawaja
Socialist Scholar

HUMA DILAWAR'S REVIEW

As I read From Wonder to Wisdom, I am filled with a quiet, profound joy that only a mother can truly comprehend. To witness my daughter Eden's thoughts and voice woven through the fabric of these pages feels nothing short of miraculous. Though she is just sixteen, within these conversations, she exists outside of time. Her curiosity is fearless, her honesty disarming, and her depth of thought illuminates each page with a grace that moves me deeply.

And then there is Dr. Khalid Sohail a philosopher, healer, and poet whose wisdom has been honed through decades of reflection. The dialogue between them is not merely an exchange of words; it is an encounter between generations, between questions and the silences that hold their answers, between wonder and wisdom.

As a mother, I have always tried to listen to Eden not only to her words, but to the spaces between them. I have tried to honour the fullness of her inner world. Yet, in this book, she has been heard in a way that feels rare and precious. Dr. Sohail did not simply speak to her, he truly conversed with her. In doing so, he offered her the sacred space to unfurl, to question, and to articulate her emerging truths.

This book is far more than a creative endeavour, it is a living bridge. A bridge between youth and experience, between innocence and insight, between the inner child that still resides within us and the wise soul that patiently waits to be known.

I am moved beyond words. Proud, of course but also humbled. Grateful in the deepest sense.

Reading *From Wonder to Wisdom* feels like sitting beside a quiet fire on a long-forgotten evening where warmth, light, and something ancient rise gently within you, reminding you that the most meaningful conversations are those that reach across time.

~Huma Dilawar
Graphic Designer, Writer

~*~

HAMID ABDUL'S REVIEW

Dear Eden

Most high school students are still figuring out the basics of life. But Eden Khawaja is different. You already understand deep subjects like psychology, philosophy, art, science, and society. Your thinking is far beyond your age. Reading your work feels like listening to someone much older and wiser.

Eden's talent didn't come from nowhere. You grew up in a home where ideas are shared and respected. Your parents clearly passed on their love for learning and truth.

Then there is Dr. Khalid Sohail, a respected psychologist and a finest human being. I've read many of his articles on HumSub. His writing helped me understand things I was confused about for years. He explains difficult ideas in a clear and honest way. Thank you Dr. Khalid Sohail.

As for me—*Hamid Uncle*—I'm not an expert. I'm not a philosopher or psychologist. I once tried reading Sartre but couldn't finish it. The only psychology book I partly understood was *Nafsiyat Kya Hai?*, by Dr. Ajmal in my college days.

When you, Zubair Khawaja Sahib, and Syeda Huma sent me your writings, I was honoured—but also nervous. I understood maybe 10% at first. After reading it three times (and using ChatGPT to understand terminology and ideas behind technicalities), I understood about half. But even when I didn't fully understand, I was amazed by Eden's thinking.

At the end of each chapter/ letter, I wrote short comments in red. They are just thoughts from a simple reader and a lay-man. If they don't match the ideas, please forgive me.

This experience gave me two gifts:

o A deeper respect for Dr. Khalid Sohail, who helped clear many old doubts in my mind through his writings.

o And great admiration for you Eden, whose mind is truly special and she is decades ahead of her time.

May you keep asking questions, thinking deeply, and sharing her light with the world.

Thank you!

~Hamid Abdul
Artist and Graphic Designer

~*~

SAJJAD HUSSAIN'S REVIEW

Dear Zubair and Eden,

I must confess, I've never been asked to write a review of a creative work before. So when Zubair asked me to share a few thoughts, I honestly wasn't sure where to begin. It took me a couple of days just to convince myself that he was serious—it almost felt like a joke at first! But when I received his follow-up message yesterday, I realized he genuinely wanted my thoughts, and that gave me the push to sit down and give the writing a proper read.

Although I haven't made it all the way through yet, I can already tell that my upcoming weekend is going to be well spent with this wonderful piece. From what I've read so far—starting with Eden's review and moving through the thoughtful narrative—it is truly captivating and refreshing. The writing draws you in and makes you feel as though you're sitting in a warm circle of friends, sharing moments filled with heartfelt conversation, serious reflections, and light-hearted joy.

Eden's questions reminded me so much of my own daughter, Reeba, who is now eight years old. I remember driving her home from school a couple of years ago when she suddenly asked, "Daddy, do you think God exists?" Before I could respond, she followed up with, "If God made the world, who made God?" I was amazed to hear such deep questions coming from a child so young. Reading this piece brought those memories back with a smile.

Gruncle's dream of becoming a doctor also felt familiar—especially for those of us raised in South Asian households where children often grow up with expectations to become doctors or engineers. (As an aside, I won't mention "lawyer" in that list—just to avoid sounding self-referential, since I happen to work as an attorney!)

Just two days ago, Reeba and I were talking about starting a bedtime reading tradition, and we discussed what book we should begin with. After reading this piece, I truly believe it would make a lovely choice for us to share. I'll be looking forward to seeing it in book form, so Reeba and I can enjoy it together—page by page.

Thanks to both writers. Your writing is not only a joy to read but also a reminder of the beauty in thoughtful storytelling and the curious, imaginative minds. Keep writing—your words have a lasting impact.

~ Sajjad Hussain
Attorney; Member - State Bar of California

KIANNA FULTON'S REVIEW

When Eden first told me about this book, I knew it would be something special. I've had so many deep and mind-bending conversations with her over the years, and I've always been amazed by how naturally she thinks about the big questions most of us are too scared or too distracted to ask. But *From Wonder to Wisdom* still surprised me. It's more than a book. It's a conversation that feels timeless.

What makes this so powerful is how real it is. These aren't polished essays or scripted interviews. They're emails. Simple, honest exchanges between Eden and Dr. Sohail that flow with curiosity, vulnerability, and respect. And somehow, that simplicity gives the book its magic. You're not just reading their words. You feel like you're there, sitting quietly beside them, listening.

Eden's questions are incredible. They're thoughtful and brave, sometimes even raw. You can feel her searching, not for the "right" answer, but for something true. And what I love is that she's not trying to sound smart or impressive. She's just being herself. And she is someone who sees the world through a deeply sensitive and intelligent lens.

Dr. Sohail responds with such kindness and depth. He doesn't rush to explain things or overcomplicate them. He listens, reflects, and shares from a place of genuine care. You can tell he sees Eden not just as a student or a younger person, but as an equal in the conversation. That mutual respect is felt on every page.

One of the most moving parts of the book for me was how it bridges so many things that usually feel far apart. A teenager and a psychologist. Two people from different generations and cultural backgrounds. And yet, through their exchange, those gaps disappear. What you're left with is something beautifully human.

It also reminded me that there's real value in slowing down. In asking questions and not rushing to answer them. In sitting with uncertainty and letting it teach you something. This book invites you into that space. It doesn't hand you solutions. It gives you permission to wonder.

As someone who knows Eden personally, I just want to say how proud I am. She's always had this way of seeing the world that's rare. Reading her words in this book, and seeing how Dr. Sohail engages with them, made me emotional more than once. Not just because I know her, but because the conversation feels so alive and meaningful.

From Wonder to Wisdom isn't a book you race through. It's one you sit with. And if you let it, it'll stay with you long after you've read the last page.

Eden, you've always been someone who makes people think and feel in ways they didn't expect. This book is such a beautiful example of that. Please keep asking questions. The world needs more voices like yours.

~Kianna Fulton
Close Friend of Co-Author Eden Khawaja

DR. PAUL WOZNIAK'S REVIEW

Dear Eden

I have begun to read the book you have written and am struck by your level of honesty and authenticity in your writing.

It is amazing that you are coming to terms and accepting your authentic self. Your courage is admirable.

~ *Dr. Paul Wozniak M.D*
Clinical Psychiatrist

DR. MOZAFFAR SIDDIQUI'S REVIEW

I was inspired when your father shared the introduction of your book with me. Excellent work and many successes in the days ahead.

~ *Dr. Mozaffar Siddiqui M.D. FRCPC*
Neorology

DR. FOUZIA SAEED'S REVIEW

From Wonder to Wisdom is a gift to young and old readers alike.

The topics discussed were very relevant to issues and stages in everyone's life. The two authors, with their very different backgrounds and ages, presented a range of perspectives on these topics. The range included very heart-felt, experiential dimensions of life nestled in technical and academic discussions, backgrounds, and classifications.

All discussions are handled in a way that helps us articulate and affirm our own questions, challenges, and unresolved issues, and helps us make sense of our lives from broader perspectives. This invariably leads to insights and resolutions within.

While Dr. Sohail is an established author, Eden's exploration of these themes at this young age is an inspiration to younger readers. It encourages them to see life itself is an educational experience. It teaches the reader how to turn our life experiences, our happiness, our sadness, our longings, everything into a growing, learning, and educational opportunity. It shows us how education is not restricted to classrooms and universities. Life teaches us, if we are open to it.

In my own work with designing educational curricula, classes, and trainings, I always paid attention to the different ways in which people learn concepts, practical skills, and go through attitudinal change. It is important not to just desire happiness in life but to turn whatever happens to us in life into learning and growing experiences. That makes life precious. This book helps us see life in that way.

The younger readers will be encouraged to first learn from their own life experiences and then become leaders in the larger society. They will not only have insights for themselves but make life an educational experience for others they end up working with over the years. I strongly encourage younger adults to read this book as it will enrich their own lives and help them to become leader and influencers in society.

From Wonder to Wisdom creates ripples that will go far.

~*Dr. Fouzia Saeed*
Author of Taboo: The Hidden Culture of a Red Light Area;
Social Scientist

GIULIA MUBEEN 'S REVIEW

In a time where we are often quick to jump to conclusions, where we claim to have answers to the inner workings of an upside down world, it is refreshing to read an exchange between two beings; who are brought together out of genuine interest, curiosity and questioning for each other and their environment.

There is something extremely poetic about asking questions that are born out of the human need to ponder, even more so when the questions come from two different generations.

The intercultural nuances and generational gaps only immerse the reader more into each individual's experience and allow us to share in their story. A girl's wondering about the future becomes mirrored by a grown man's own personal trajectory. The simplicity of the email questions and responses between the two becomes a very powerful portal which considers what it means to be human.

I found the book an inspiring entry which comments on each of our intricate life tapestries, whilst unmasking how the same threads and fabrics may be woven across generations, to create the timeless tapestry of humanity.

There is poetry in this structure, not only in the rhythm of the language, but in the form itself. The act of correspondence, slow and intentional, reminds us of the beauty in waiting, in receiving, in crafting language not as noise, but as offering. In a world that clamours for answers, From Wonder to Wisdom dares to dwell in the question.

As someone who lives the experience of another generation, born in a multicultural sphere, the questions that were asked by Eden, a distant cousin that I have not yet had the pleasure to meet, sparked a feeling of closeness that transcends all questions. Instead, it unites us in a feeling that we all, in the end, are not too dissimilar.

~ Giulia Mubeen
International Relations Masters Student
Prague, Czech Republic

TOLTU TUFA'S REVIEW

Reading Eden's book offered a special glimpse into a living and breathing conversation we rarely see between generations. I enjoyed being invited to the conversing minds of an emerging adolescent and a seasoned adult exploring life, meaning, and identity. To me, the letters between Eden and her "Gruncle" are both personal and philosophical, and what stands out is their genuine connection with one another.

Eden's voice is reflective, questioning and while sometimes vulnerable, she is driven by a desire to understand herself and the world around her. This book does not try to offer neat answers. Instead, it shows what can happen when two people across generations make space for real, respectful conversation.

It's tender, wise, and quietly powerful; a gift to those believing in the power of conversations that build across generations.

~ Toltu Tufa
Author and Psychologist

DR. KAMRAN AHMAD'S REVIEW

Eden Khawaja and Dr. Khalid Sohail take a deep dive into issues ranging from personal to universal. Dr. Khalid Sohail's style remains personal and anecdotal, pulling out deeper insights and wisdom from his life experiences and reflections, enriched by his studies and readings of the wisdom traditions. Eden starts with a very personal and revelatory voice and then switches to an intellectual, analytical, and philosophical tone that summarizes studies and theories, ideologies and perspectives, both historically and universally.

Dr. Khalid Sohail has about 80 or so books to his name and this is the first book for Eden Khawaja. I always enjoy interdisciplinary exchanges, but this one is a dialogue between writers who are two generations apart and tremendously different in so many other ways. That makes it a pleasure, especially in the beginning of the dialogue, where the tone remains more personal.

There is something in this book for everyone. There are opportunities for individual growth and insights from reading the personal experiences and learnings of both the authors. There are also opportunities to learn from the range of intellectual ideas presented over the exchange.

What we take from the exchange as readers depends on what we are looking for in this book and in life. The book presents a rich exchange that can stimulate ideas, experiences, and growth on many levels, both consciously and unconsciously.

I congratulate both authors on the completion of this unusual exchange.

~Dr. Kamran Ahmad
Author, Clinical Psychologist

AFSHEEN'S REVIEW

A Glimmer of Soul

A luminous exchange,

where Eden's spirit,

young yet ancient,

meets a sage's soft gleam

Not words, but light,

a passage between souls.

Her sixteen years,

a boundless grace,

stars igniting within...

My heart swells

with a love unbounded..

A quiet fire,

truths beautifully cast..

For her, and for him

a pure marvel

~ Afsheen

ABOUT THE AUTHORS

Dr. Khalid Sohail, psychiatrist, poet, and writer, has a wide range of interests and passions. He received his degree in medicine from Khyber Medical College, Pakistan in 1974, and completed his residency in Psychiatry at Memorial University, Newfoundland in 1982. From 1983 to 1995 he worked in psychiatric hospitals in Newfoundland, New Brunswick and Ontario. In 1995 he left the hospital to open the Creative Psychotherapy Clinic in Whitby, Ontario. He has presented papers at professional conferences in various countries.

Whether through the written word or the moving image, Dr. Sohail has always been interested in sharing his humanistic philosophy about people suffering from mental illness and emotional problems, with other professionals, family members and the community at large. He also believes that learning is a life-long process, and that working together is better than working alone.

Eden Khawaja, is a sixteen-year-old high school student whose thoughtful voice adds a fresh and powerful perspective to From Wonder to Wisdom. At just fifteen, she was awarded the United Nations Young Leader Certificate, recognizing her early commitment to global awareness and youth leadership.

Eden's writing is shaped by a deep sense of curiosity, compassion, and a desire to engage meaningfully with the world. Her contributions to this book reflect not only the wonder of a young mind exploring big ideas, but also the emerging wisdom of a generation unafraid to speak up, reflect deeply, and imagine boldly. Through her lens, readers are invited to rediscover timeless questions and perhaps see them anew.

Wisdom is the inner light that helps us see in the dark.

~Sohail

www.ingramcontent.com/pod-product-compliance
Lightning Source LLC
Chambersburg PA
CBHW030408020726
47493CB00003B/983